MW01504776

IT NEVER HAPPENED

CARLEY WOLFE

ISBN: 9798385986316

Cover Design: Olivia Pro Design
Editing: Sarah Hawkins

First Print Edition: 2023
First Electronic Edition: 2023

For Susie

PART ONE

1

Ella
April 25, 2022

"Hey, Ry," Ella called into her car's Bluetooth. She straightened in the seat of her silver SUV and checked her makeup in the rearview mirror. The sight of her pale skin made her mouth twist. She needed to get a tan, desperately. Meticulously, she smoothed out a few flyways from her blonde bob before focusing back on the road.

"Toad." His voice was low and sensual even coming from the car's speakers. She could make out that he too was in his car, probably on his way to his first showing of the day. Whenever he used his pet name for her, she melted a little inside, even after eighteen years of marriage. The running joke had been that he was a prince charming, and rather than a frog prince, she was the frog princess. Self-demeaning humor was a skill she had picked up from her mother and had carried with her into the relationship with her husband. Everybody else cringed when they heard it, but Ella still loved it.

"What's up?" She pulled up to a stoplight and glanced over at Charlie's, a coffee shop on the corner. Her mouth suddenly felt dry as she contemplated grabbing a quick caffeine fix and maybe even a chocolate croissant. But one quick look at her stomach reminded her that she shouldn't. Yet another thing she picked up from her mother.

"I just dropped the kids off at school. I wanted to let you know I have a late night tonight. There's some kind of dinner with a new client. I don't know. Sam said I should be there, so . . ." Ryan's voice grew hesitant at the end, like he was waiting for her to tell him he needed to be home.

"Dinner with a client?"

Traffic had started moving again, and Ella was pulling into the doctor's office parking lot. She slammed on the brakes as she drove around to the side entrance, nearly colliding with an elderly patient. She threw her hand up and mouthed *sorry.*

"Yeah, I guess they are looking to expand into business real estate, and they want the entire firm represented. I told them that I thought it was a bit much, but—"

"It's no big deal. We'll order pizza or something." Ella felt like her nerves were on fire, which caused her to ignore the hesitancy in Ryan's voice.

"Alright." He let out a long sigh. "I guess I will go. I'll be home late. Make sure you save me a slice. The food is never good at those things."

Ella released a nervous laugh as she threw the car into park. "Yeah. I just pulled into the office so I'll talk to you later." Her finger hovered above the end-call button on the center console's display. "Oh, I forgot to tell you last night: Your dry cleaning is in the hallway closet. I got caught up doing stuff and forgot to take it upstairs."

"The one with the navy suit?"

"Yup. I figured you might want to wear your *lucky* suit tonight," Ella teased while she tapped her car door with her left hand. Her French manicure glimmered in the morning sunlight.

"Of course, I'm gonna wear it. I'll swing by home after lunch to grab it. Thanks, babe."

"I'll see you tonight. Love you." She pressed the end-call button just as Ryan started to say it back. Work started in five minutes, and she was usually situated at her desk by now. She reached across the passenger seat and grabbed her black leather bag before stepping out of the SUV and onto the damp pavement. Her sneakers squeaked against the tile floor as she entered the back of the office.

"Morning, Lexi," Ella called as she moved into the staff room to set down her purse. She grabbed her phone and carried it with her to behind the front desk before settling into her spot.

Lexi, a woman in her early twenties, sat on the other end of the circular desk, shoveling wild berry yogurt into her mouth.

"Eww!" she exclaimed as she pulled a piece of her own brown hair from her mouth.

"That's what happens when you eat too fast," Ella scolded, chuckling to herself as she booted up her computer.

"Okay, Mom." Lexi rolled her eyes, and Ella felt a blush come over her cheeks. She knew Lexi was only joking, but it was a stark reminder of their age difference. Over twenty years were between them, and Ella could easily be Lexi's mother.

"Do anything fun last weekend?" Ella asked after clearing her throat.

"I had a date with some guy at a new bar downtown." Lexi shrugged, but Ella leaned forward a bit, eager for a taste of the carefree spirit she no longer possessed. "Bar was a hit. Guy was a dud."

Ella smiled and shook her head. "They can't all be princes."

"Gag." Ella had told Lexi about Ryan's pet name for her a few months ago when he had called in to ask her a question about their new life insurance policy. "I can't believe you let him call you that. First of all, it's a gross name, and second, it's super cheesy."

Ella grinned as she grabbed the keys out of her desk drawer and got up to unlock the front of the office so patients could begin to come in. Since it was Monday, they would have lots of people calling in about mysterious ailments they had fallen victim to over the weekend. Why these people never used urgent care, she wasn't sure.

Ella caught a glimpse of herself in the reflection of the door. Even in her blue, loose scrubs, she couldn't really hide all the parts of herself she hated. Instead, she tried looking at her smile, which always had been her favorite quality. Maybe, if she pretended hard enough, the rest didn't matter.

Lexi glanced out the front window as Ella turned the key in the lock. "Looks like it's going to be gross out later." Within seconds, Lexi had the weather pulled up on her phone. "Thunderstorms. Maybe hail." She shrugged and ate another spoonful of yogurt.

"It always storms like this in April." Ella settled back down at her desk and sent a quick text to both her children, Nate and Sophia, warning them that it may be downpouring when they walk home later.

2

Tiana
April 25, 2022

"How uncomfortable do you feel in this room, right now?" Tiana Hill leaned slightly forward in her chair, her slender legs crossed, her left elbow resting on her thigh and supporting her. Her brown curls swayed as she moved. The large woman before her swallowed, her eyes darting across the office.

"Very uncomfortable." There was a slight shake to her voice. The woman had tucked the tips of her hands under her thighs.

"On a scale from one to ten: one being mostly comfortable and ten being you want to burst into tears and leave immediately." Tiana let a friendly smile creep onto her lips. She loved her work, particularly when she reached the second session with a new client. If the patient was willing and open, it was like she could get a glimpse directly inside their brains. She got to see the world as they did.

"Ten." A single tear ran down the woman's left cheek, leaving a large dark splotch on her bright pink t-shirt. Without conscious thought, Tiana reached over to the coffee table and held out a tissue box. The woman took a single tissue. Tiana's arm remained extended. After a moment, the woman took two more, just as more tears began to fall.

"Ten. Wow." Tiana settled back into her armchair, smoothing out her white silk blouse. She took just a moment to admire the contrast it made with her golden-brown skin. It was a combination she had always loved. The woman opposite her nodded vehemently. "I think we need to discuss that number, though. You are here, and you got through your first session. You came back for a second one, even though you feel uncomfortable. That makes you strong and brave. That takes a lot of courage. The fact is, though, you aren't leaving, are you?"

"No," the woman squeaked before blowing her nose.

"So, what number do you think you *really* are at right now, in this very moment?" Tiana's head tilted to the right, taking in the picture as a whole. The woman clutched the dirtied tissues to her chest. Her once pale face was now bright red. For just a split second, Tiana thought how grateful she was that the couch was leather and could be wiped down easily.

"An eight?"

Tiana smiled, but without her bright teeth. "Are you asking me or telling me?" Her voice was stern but it still had a softness to it. She needed to be encouraging but firm with these sorts of patients.

"An eight." The woman gave a little nod before letting out a hiccup. Her hand flew to her mouth and her face became red all over again. "I'm sorry."

"It's okay!" Tiana let herself chuckle, and the woman gave herself permission to laugh as well. They were building a relationship that Tiana knew would make the work over the next few sessions so much easier.

The session carried on as per usual, without any major breakthroughs or discoveries. Tiana learned that her patient's issues stemmed from an unstable childhood, where her parents often changed their moods at the drop of a hat. It was a story Tiana had heard many times before. It made her grateful for her own father, who raised her mostly on his own and did a good job at that.

They were scheduled to meet again in a week. As the woman left Tiana's home—the majority of the first floor of her home had been converted to an office— the rain started to tumble down from the skies, soaking everything. Just as the high school down the road was dismissing.

3

Ella
April 25, 2022

Ella was putting away some physical copies of patient files when five thirty rolled around. Dr. Wagner, the primary physician at the practice, insisted they keep paper files just in case. Ella was standing in the back office when she heard the front door open. All their patients were already accounted for, and there weren't any deliveries scheduled. The storm had come just like Lexi's weather app had predicted, and a deluge of rain had surrounded them. It was tapering off but still periodically raining. She had a few left when Lexi called out to her.

"Ella!"

The panic in Lexi's voice made her stomach drop. Ella's mind flashed through the possibilities. A robbery. A person with a severe injury who somehow arrived at the conclusion that a family practice would be able to stitch them up. Ella bit her bottom lip and hugged the files to her chest. She stepped out of the back office.

Two police officers stood in uniform at the front desk. As to be expected, they were soaked. They were both muscular, younger officers, one of them sporting a rather unflattering mustache. Ella hated mustaches, and for a moment, she allowed herself to be transfixed by his, knowing it was better than thinking about what was coming next. Because somehow, she knew.

"They want to talk to you." The words spilled out of Lexi's mouth as she stood awkwardly behind the desk, clearly unsure what to do with herself in this situation.

"Mrs. Thomas?" the clean-shaven one asked. Ella allowed herself to peek at his name tag. Reynolds. She wondered if he had a family. Her eyes flicked to the second officer. Smith.

"Yes. That's me." She set down the files in the middle of the desk, swallowing hard. Already she was feeling light-headed.

"You may want to sit down." Smith forced his hands into his pockets.

Ella shook her head.

"I'm fine right here." Her words were stern, offering no room for disagreement. The second detective shrugged and looked away.

"Mrs. Thomas, I'm afraid there has been an incident."

Ella thought hard about his word choice. Incident. Not an accident. An incident seemed worse.

"Go on." She could already feel the sobs through her body like phantom pains, preparing for what he would say next.

"Your husband is deceased."

Ella blinked. Never in her wildest imagination did she imagine those words to come next. She assumed it would be Nate. Her brain even went so far as to think maybe he threatened someone at school. Maybe he considered bringing a gun. But never did she think it would be Ryan.

"How?" Ella found herself sitting down, gripping the armrests of her chair firmly. Her knuckles turned white.

"Your children discovered him at home in your bedroom. He had already passed when they arrived."

Ella imagined poor Sophia discovering her father's body, and tears swallowed her violently. Lexi approached and rubbed Ella's back in small, circular motions. Ella grabbed a tissue from the desk and wiped at her nose. She forced herself to catch her breath.

"Was it a heart attack?" Ella had always worried that eating fast food on the way to all those house showings would eventually catch up to him. And he spent so much time sitting. He was a relatively healthy weight, and he exercised in his free time, but cholesterol always caught up with men.

"At this point, we aren't certain what it was." Reynolds frowned and looked at his partner, who avoided eye contact with Ella.

"I guess it could have been anything." She frowned, choking back more tears. "Aneurysm, stroke, anything."

"Mrs. Thomas"—Reynolds paused to clear his throat—"They are still investigating the scene, but they haven't ruled it accidental."

"What?" Ella glanced over at Lexi as though she hadn't heard him right. Unfortunately, Lexi looked just as confused as she did.

"There are a few things that have raised suspicion that perhaps"—Reynolds cleared his throat again—"it may be ruled a homicide."

"But who would kill him?"

For a brief moment, Ella wondered if they were here not only to tell her the news, but to question her as a possible suspect. She and Ryan had watched countless episodes of *Dateline*, and it was almost always the husband. Which meant it could just as well be the wife.

"The investigators have some questions about that, too, but they figured you would want to see your children as soon as possible. They plan to meet with you tomorrow."

Ella stood and nodded. "Yes." She pulled in a slow, shaky breath. "I need to see the kids. I need to get home." She didn't feel like she was entirely in her own body. Instead, she was staring off into the distance, unable to focus her vision.

"Ma'am." Smith moved toward the desk and held out his hand, silently warning her to stop.

"I need to see my kids." Ella turned to Lexi. "I need my purse. I need my phone." Ella's eyes scanned the desk but came up empty. Lexi reached over and picked up the phone from right next to Ella's keyboard, where she always kept it.

"I'll go get your purse." A few tears fell down Lexi's cheeks as she left the room.

"Your kids are at the police station. Obviously, your home is a crime scene. We will need to keep the house closed off for tonight, and you will have to stay elsewhere." Smith looked sternly at Ella. "Do you understand?"

Ella bit her bottom lip. "No. None of this makes

sense." She collapsed back into the chair and put her face in her hands. *This isn't real. This isn't happening.*

4

Tiana
April 25, 2022

At quarter to three, Tiana climbed into her black Mercedes, the hem of her navy dress pants getting soaked. She cursed herself for not parking in the garage the day before. She set up her phone to call Sophia just as she backed out of the driveway and headed toward the high school. She thought she would probably be able to catch the kids on the sidewalk, heading home, but it was impossible to see their faces with so many umbrellas and hoodies. Her eyes darted to her phone, which went straight to voicemail. She smashed the end-call button as she turned into the Franklin High School parking lot.

"You try to do something nice and this is where it gets you," Tiana groaned as she parked at the front entrance of the school. She knew Sophia frequently stayed after school for clubs, but Nate was not the extracurricular type.

Tiana pulled down the sun visor and checked her hair in the mirror. Frizz was already developing in her curls. She scrunched her nose, her dark freckles moving closer together.

Tiana flipped to her favorites, finding the contact for Nate. She remembered getting his number when he got his first phone. Her number was the only one he had memorized, apart from all the immediate family that had been present when he opened it. With the way Nate went through cell phones, she was shocked Ella still let him have one, but she hit call anyway.

It rang three times before Nate's voice came across the line.

"Hey, Aunt T!" His voice was enthusiastic, which set off alarm bells. He was not an excitable teen. Brooding would be a better word.

"Hey . . ." She forgot why she had been calling for a moment. "I was just calling to see if you and Sophia wanted a ride home from school. I'm in the parking lot now." She could hear the sound of another voice in the background. It was muffled, but she thought it might be Sophia.

"No, we're good, thanks!"

Tiana blinked.

"Did someone else give you a ride home?"

Tiana knew that Ella did not like the two of them riding in other people's cars, especially without them knowing about it. While it was a possibility that they had gotten permission, she had a bad feeling about it. There was more muffled conversation in the background.

"Nathaniel Matthew, what is going on here?"

The muffled voices stopped instantly.

"What do you mean?"

Tiana rolled her eyes and crossed her arms involuntarily. "You know what I mean. First of all, you never are this polite or excited to talk to anyone. Now, if you have had some kind of life-altering epiphany, that's one thing, but I'm betting my money that it's something other than that."

Nate cleared his throat on the other side of the line.

"Sophia and I are together, and I just bet her that if she didn't answer, you would call me next. She owes me ten bucks now."

"So, you made a bet on me?" Tiana feigned offense, but really, she knew the kids were good-natured—most of the time. It also boosted her ego a bit that the kids knew her so well, despite the fact that she wasn't actually their aunt.

"Yeah. But we don't need a ride. We are staying after school."

"Both of you?" One of Tiana's perfectly manicured eyebrows raised in suspicion. The phone was jostled and then Sophia's voice came over the line.

"I'm helping him study for the state tests. There's a tutoring session, and I'm going to make sure he pays attention."

Tiana smiled. "Okay. Well, I'll head home then, but call me if you need a ride later. This storm doesn't look like it's stopping anytime soon."

"Of course!" Sophia said. "Love you!"

Tiana thought she could even hear Nate's voice echoing Sophia's words, too, albeit they were more of a grumble than anything.

"Love you both." Tiana ended the call and put her car back into drive. She couldn't explain why there was a pit in her stomach.

5

Ella
April 25, 2022

When Ella arrived at the police station around six p.m., she expected her children, or at least Sophia, to run into her arms like when they were kids. Instead, they sat in the interrogation room, side by side and silent. Sophia was picking some dirt out from under her nails. Both of them were sporting jeans. Sophia had on the t-shirt with a quote from her favorite television show that they had bought for her for Christmas. Ella couldn't remember what it was called. Nate, as always, had his black hoodie pulled up over his head, and he was playing with the strings as Ella looked through the glass.

"We will probably need to question all of you tomorrow." Reynolds fidgeted around, appearing unsure of what to do with his hands. Ella wondered if he wanted to pat her shoulder. She was glad he decided not to. Her mouth formed a tight line, emphasizing the wrinkles on her face. If she had lived a different lifestyle, she might have gotten fillers to stop herself from aging. Instead, she stared in the mirror for hours, fixating on the places where her skin didn't cooperate. Where it caved in or rose up like a mountain, making her feel insecure.

"I want to be in the room." Ella didn't take her eyes off her children.

"Understood. Would you like to go in now?" Reynolds rested his hand on the doorknob, relieved to finally have something to do. Ella gave a small nod, and he opened the door.

Sophia glanced up at her mother and then immediately back down. She had the dirty blonde hair that Ella used to have before she bleached it all out. It rested in a bun at the top of her head. She seemed so small in comparison to her brother. He looked like a full-grown adult, minus the stubble on his face that never really grew in right, even though he was only seventeen. Sophia, one year younger, seemed diminutive compared to him.

Ella had expected Sophia to be crying, but her face appeared dry. Nate, however, had a few wet spots on his hoodie. Ella stopped in the doorway and took in the scene for a moment. Nate's eyes looked up to meet his mother's gaze, and his face was splotchy. The last time he had cried in front of her, he had been a preteen.

"Mom." Nate forced the words out and nudged his sister, who sat as if she was in a daze. Sophia looked at him and then at Ella.

"Hi." Sophia's voice was so soft, Ella could barely hear her.

"Hi guys," Ella whispered back. Nate stood up abruptly from his chair, the metal scraping against the floor. For a brief moment, Ella felt afraid.

"I'm so sorry, Mom." Nate closed the distance between them and wrapped his arms around Ella tightly. After a second, she wrapped her arms around him too. She couldn't remember the last hug she had gotten from her son. He gripped her tightly, her face pressed against his chest and shoulder. She rubbed his back.

"It's okay." Her voice shook, betraying her. Just over his right shoulder, Ella could see Sophia still sitting in the chair, her eyes appearing to stare a million miles away.

Shock, Ella thought. That was what was wrong with her lovely child. In a way, she wondered if Nate was in shock, too, which was why he was being so affectionate. When she remembered that they had been the ones to discover Ryan's body, she fell apart, her own tears mixing with Nate's on his hoodie. He gripped her tighter, and it was exactly what she needed.

6

Tiana
April 25, 2022

After arriving home from her unsuccessful school pickup, Tiana decided it would be an early night for her. She always booked herself heavy with clients in the morning so she could keep her afternoons open for whatever she wanted. While it gave her the freedom to have her own exciting life, she never seemed to be able to put the pieces in place to make it happen.

On the second floor of her home, which was where everything was with the exception of the kitchen and the dining room (her office took up quite a bit of space), she drew a warm bath and selected a sage-green silk pajama set. Tiana lovingly ran her fingers over the silk and let out a long sigh before deciding tonight was one of those nights that she would need some wine. Wrapped in a cotton bathrobe monogrammed with her initials, part of a 40th birthday gift from Ella, Tiana made her way down to the first floor to pour herself a glass of rosé. Her dog, Ollie, jumped down from her bed to follow her downstairs, not wanting to be left to his own devices. He easily kept pace despite missing an entire hind leg. She reached down and ran her fingers lazily over his head.

"Good boy." Ollie moved his head to quickly lick her fingers, and she withdrew them. "I know where your mouth has been," she reminded him. He looked away, avoiding eye contact. Ollie had been adopted a few years ago. Despite wanting a classic guard dog, Tiana immediately fell in love with the dog Sophia had found while volunteering at the local animal shelter. He was a mix of all different breeds, and the only thing he could really intimidate was a rabbit.

The floors creaked a bit as she made her way down them. The house, while it looked newly built on the inside, had old bones. Tiana had fallen in love with the house back when she lived in Seattle. A friend from high school worked in real estate in Texas and had posted the listing on Facebook. Instantly, Tiana was in love. The brick edifice of the home combined with the surrounding greenery reminded Tiana of a Jane Austen novel. Tiana had never read any Austen, but the comparison felt right inside her head. She hadn't even spent time looking at where the home was before sending a message to the realtor. Within a month, she had closed on the home and had moved all of her belongings despite the protests of her loving father. She distinctly remembered an argument, if she could even call it that, they had a week before she left.

"Sweetie, it's a big decision. And I don't want you to be alone. You've never been out on your own."

It had been true. She had lived almost all of her life with her father or just around the corner from him. But some tiny voice inside her was screaming she needed to get away.

"Come with me then. There's nothing stopping you!"

Her father was happily retired, and he had no financial obligations that kept him in one place. His career as a teacher had left him with a nice pension, which had been one of the few benefits apart from summers off with his daughter.

"I can't. There's too much life for me here." Her father gestured grandly around the apartment, but Tiana's eyes stopped on the photographs scattered across every flat surface in the home. Her father with his coworkers at his retirement party. The little league baseball team he coached last year proudly holding a participation trophy. There were a dozen photographs of him with people all across the town. He had a natural inclination toward making friends. And while it wouldn't be hard for him to do it again in Texas, Tiana understood why he wouldn't want to leave it all behind.

"And I can't stay." Her voice had been soft. She reached out and grabbed his hand with both of hers, her thumb running across the back of his hand, just as he had done to her when she was younger. Her father had nodded, despite a few tears gathering at the edges of his eyes, and eventually gave her a small smile.

"I know you'll do great things wherever you go."

And that was the end of it. They never talked about her decision again, but they had phone calls twice a week where they discussed the amazing life he was living and some of her successes as well. She often had much less to say than he did, but he never asked if she was unhappy. She never did feel unhappy or regret the decision until he had passed away nine years ago. A little guilt had washed over her that she wasn't there for his last days, but knowing he was surrounded by so many people who loved him helped her heal faster.

By the time she returned to the bathtub with her wine, it was nearly overflowing with bubbles.

"Shit," Tiana cursed under her breath as she scrambled to shut it off. "Today is not my day, huh?" She glanced at Ollie, who had settled down on the rug in front of the sink. He was already licking himself in ways that made Tiana cringe.

7

Ella
April 25, 2022

"You're pretty quiet back there," Ella called. Sophia met her mother's eyes in the rearview window. Nate sat in the passenger seat per usual, and Sophia, the shortest, was relegated to the back.

"What is there to say?" Sophia's voice cracked halfway through the sentence. It was the first complete sentence she had spoken since Ella met them at the station. Sophia turned to face back out the window. Her daughter had begun to develop a tan from spending time on their back patio doing her homework since the weather started warming up. Freckles were scattered across her face, something she had inherited from Ryan.

Ella grimaced and stared back out the front windshield, turning onto their street on autopilot.

"Alright, when we get inside, I'll grab the suitcases from the basement . . ."

Nate reached over and touched his mother's arm. "We aren't going on vacation. They said it would only be a night or two, max."

Ella swallowed and nodded. She pulled into the driveway and let out a deep breath. Ella had always thought their beige home looked warm and welcoming: a flower garden out front, two-car garage, and a little sign on the front door with their last name. Now, she only felt dread when she looked at it. Despite it still being daylight, the entire two-story house had the lights on. Clearly, detectives were still working on the scene.

Finally, she took a long look at Nate. She wasn't sure what was more shocking: the death of her husband or her irresponsible son becoming the voice of reason.

Every time Ella looked at Nate, she saw him as she had five years ago. She had left work early because she hadn't been feeling well. As she was driving home, she got stopped at a traffic light just before the main drag of town branched off into housing developments. Right next to Sal's Convenience Store, she saw two boys standing in the alleyway. What had grabbed her attention wasn't the boys, but the flames coming from the trash can. Ella had glanced back at the stoplight and saw that it was still red. Her eyes darted back, and the flames lit up the boys' faces. One of them was Nate.

Ella inhaled sharply and pulled off into the turning lane, throwing on her hazards. She was so shocked that when she got out of the car, she nearly forgot to shut her door.

"Nathaniel!" Ella screeched as she approached. Her son looked up at her and panic crossed his eyes. His head swiveled from side to side, probably looking for somewhere to run, but the alleyway was a dead end, blocked by a large dumpster. It didn't really matter, though, because she had seen him, and there was no going back.

Once she had dragged her son back into the car, she was silent, afraid of what she would say. Partially because she believed she must have done something terribly wrong for her young son to not only skip school but to also light fires near buildings. Her mind flicked through all the true crime she had watched over the years, and she knew that statistically, children who played with fire did not have promising futures.

Nate refused to look at her, instead staring down at his dark-wash jeans.

Unable to take the silence any longer, she opened her mouth.

"What would possess you to do something like that?" She glanced over at Nate, trying to keep control of herself as she drove home. He frowned and didn't respond. "Nathaniel!" Her voice cracked as she shouted his name.

"I'm sorry." That was all he ever said about that day.

"Mom," Nate said. He touched her arm, pulling Ella back into reality. They were in the driveway, and her husband was dead.

"Sorry," she said, shaking off the bad memory of her son.

"We need to go in. The cops are waiting."

Ella's eyes darted up to the front door. A plainclothes officer stood in the doorway of their home. She swallowed hard and pushed open the car door.

"Just the essentials, right?" She glanced back at Sophia, but she had already climbed out of the car.

"Do you want me to go in and get stuff for you?" Nate offered.

Ella bit her bottom lip. It was tempting to avoid having to go into the house, but the idea of Nate sorting through her panties made her stomach churn.

"It's all right." She forced herself out of the car, a little surprised when her legs actually held up her weight. For a moment, she felt ashamed of herself. Here she was, unable to cope, when her own children had been the ones to find her husband's corpse. Nate was taking it in stride, but she knew Sophia was struggling, even if she was silent. Both of them were putting on a better act than she was though.

She took the lead, forcing herself to catch up with Sophia by the time they all reached the doorway.

"Mrs. Thomas?" the officer asked, holding out his hand. Ella reached out and shook it, tossing her shoulders back in an attempt at confidence.

"Yes." Her voice wavered out of uncertainty. She was a widow after all. Confident probably wasn't the look to go for.

"I'm Detective Clemens." He was a muscular man that Ella figured was in his early forties. His hands were calloused, and his grip was firm but not painful. Ella reached down and smoothed out her scrubs. "We are working on finding trace evidence at the moment, but we have mostly cleared your bedrooms. Unfortunately, we still need an officer to supervise you while you gather your belongings."

Two officers in full uniform appeared from the kitchen. Ella frowned, but kept her mouth shut for now.

"Would you please go with the kids to their rooms?" Clemens asked, though his tone made it clear this was not a request. Sophia turned and headed straight up toward the stairs, the officers following quickly behind. Nate took a long look at his mother before joining them.

"Why were they in my kitchen?" Ella's hands rested on her hips. She had remembered someone telling her that Ryan was found in the bedroom.

"We are doing a survey of the entire home. We only get one chance to find all the evidence, and we don't want to leave anything behind."

Ella dropped her hands from her hips and sighed. Why she felt so defensive, she wasn't sure, but something told her she needed to have her guard up.

"If you would lead the way to your room." Clemens gestured to the stairs, and Ella started up them, feeling his eyes watching all her movements. She knew that they couldn't believe it was her who had done this. She was at work all day. Her thoughts floated around in her brain until a new one popped up: *What if they think I hired someone?* The idea was laughable. What money would she use? It wasn't like she had an extra few grand to spare for a contract killer. What was the going rate for a hired hit in Texas? It couldn't be that high when its residents were practically born with a gun in hand.

Ella spun on her heels and marched herself up the stairs and to the main bedroom. An officer was posted outside the door, and he waited until Clemens caught up before opening it. The door opening felt like slow motion as more and more of her room was revealed. Her husband's body, of course, was gone, but there was blood splatter. Covering the gray carpet. The beige walls. Their floral bedspread. Ella had watched enough true crime to know this was no accident.

8

Tiana
April 25, 2022

Tiana and Ollie had settled down on the couch in her bedroom, Chinese takeout spread across the coffee table in front of her. Since she didn't have a usable living room downstairs, her bedroom was where she spent most of her time relaxing. A reality TV show played on the television, and occasionally, Tiana jeered at the cast members and their less-than-stellar life choices.

Wedged between her thigh and the armrest, her phone began to vibrate. When Tiana realized it was a call and not a text, she scrambled to retrieve it. Ella's name sat at the top of the screen, and she smiled.

"Hey, what's up?" Tiana put the phone on speaker and set it on her thigh so she could shovel some more lo mein into her mouth.

"Tiana." Ella's heavy breathing could be heard over the line. Tiana blinked and reached for the remote to mute the television. For a split second, it sounded like Ella was laughing.

"Yeah?" Tiana prompted her when no more words came.

"He's dead."

Tiana's eyes flashed back to the phone, which she snatched up and held up to her chin. She set the takeout container back on the coffee table so roughly Ollie was able to snatch a few stray noodles that had fallen onto the floor.

"Who's dead?"

Much like Ella, Tiana's first thought was Nate. Images flashed in her mind of him committing suicide, getting into a car crash with his reckless friends, or even overdosing. The last one felt the most ridiculous of all. As far as she knew, Nate had only tried pot once, and he claimed he didn't like it.

"Ryan." It was clear now that Ella was actually crying and not laughing.

"Where are you? I'll come right now." Tiana was now pacing the length of her bedroom. There had to be a mistake. She'd never known two people who were more in love than Ryan and Ella. Their relationship was what Tiana dreamed of; instead, she was stuck consuming ungodly amounts of MSG on a couch with a three-legged dog.

"Sammie's Motel." A little ounce of shame leaked into Ella's voice.

"Don't unpack. I can get you in somewhere better. Sammie's Motel. Jesus Christ." Tiana fumbled with the takeout containers and carried them to the kitchen downstairs. "Are the kids there too? Are they safe?"

"Yes . . ." Ella let out a long, slow breath.

"Just hold on. I will be there in 20."

* * *

Traffic was relatively calm since it was roughly eight o'clock. Their suburb got sleepy around seven thirty during the week, and Tiana resented it as she gripped the steering wheel so hard it hurt. Traffic would have been a welcomed distraction.

She hadn't allowed herself to cry yet. That would come later. Although Ella was the one she was close with, Ryan was always a part of the package, just like the kids. Ryan would be the one to help Tiana with the tasks around the house that she was planning on hiring a professional to do. The summer Ella and Tiana had first met, Ryan helped her paint the entire second floor of her home in various shades of cream and gray. Nate and Sophia had been there, too, but at that point, they were mostly obstructions rather than helpers.

The day Tiana had met Ella almost did bring those tears to her eyes, but she swallowed them back. Tiana was standing in line at a small, local coffee shop on the edge of town, hoping to get a quick coffee before her afternoon sessions began. At that point, seven years ago, she was still struggling to build her clientele, so she had to be flexible and let her patients make her schedule. A stout man walked into the shop, looking more like he belonged at a McDonald's getting a dollar coffee and harassing the employees about how it used to be cheaper. A teenager followed behind, and Tiana connected the dots. He was a grandpa, dragged inside by his granddaughter who just had to have her chai latte.

At that point, Tiana was third and last in line, but the man saddled up and squeezed himself in front of her. A moment went by where she debated saying anything, and her eyes glanced around the shop, where only white faces stared back. They were waiting to see what she would do.

"Excuse me, sir," Tiana said, clearing her throat when her voice came out too squeaky. The man did not turn around or seem to react at all. "Sir." Tiana reached out and lightly touched his upper arm. If Tiana had still been looking at the other spectators in the shop, she would have seen the horror on their faces, but it was too late.

The man spun around and whipped his arm away from her.

"Don't touch me."

Tiana figured that response was warranted, so she gave a small smile.

"I'm sorry. I don't think you saw that I was in line before you."

The man hooked his thumbs into his belt loops and puffed out his chest. He was a touch shorter than Tiana, hunched over by old age. His granddaughter didn't even look up from her phone.

"I saw you." His words had developed into something new. It took Tiana a second to place it. "I ain't waiting around for . . ."

Now Tiana could put her finger on it—racism. She pursed her lips, ready for the full fury of this man to be unleashed on her in a coffee shop of all places. Her father had taught her when she was younger to just let these people talk themselves into a corner. Talking back never looked good. He said it just gave them exactly what they were looking for and encouraged them to do it again.

A white woman had materialized from a nearby table, her mouth halfway open and ready to speak.

Tiana made desperate eye contact with the woman, her brain already calculating this woman's next move. Tiana shook her head from side to side.

The woman paused and took a step back, biting her bottom lip in confusion. Tiana could tell she wanted to swoop in and save the day. She'd seen it quite a few times before. While she appreciated the gesture, she would really rather not have any 'help' at all.

Tiana turned her attention back to the man in front of her, who had turned back around to face the counter. She let out a breath she had been holding onto ever since the man had pulled his arm back. After ordering her iced vanilla latte, Tiana stood by the counter, letting her eyes search for the woman who had attempted to intervene. She found her sitting in the corner, staring out the windows. She must have felt eyes on her because the woman turned to sneak a glance at Tiana. Tiana smiled, and the woman returned it. The lines on her forehead made it obvious she was worried that she had done the wrong thing.

"Iced vanilla latte!"

Tiana nodded to the barista as she grabbed her drink. Her brain jumped back and forth, trying to decide if she should say something to her new 'friend.' Before she could reach a conclusion, her legs were already carrying her to the corner.

The woman turned in her seat to face Tiana as she saw her approach. Worry lines were embedded into her forehead, and Tiana noticed her playing with the wedding ring with her right hand.

"Hey," Tiana began. "Mind if I sit?"

Ella reached over and eagerly moved her purse off the chair opposite her. "Please do!" She waited for Tiana to get settled before speaking up.

"I'm Ella." She held out her hand with a huge smile. The contagiousness of her smile rubbed off on Tiana.

"Tiana." She took a quick sip of her latte. "Thanks for trying to stand up for me back there."

Ella shook her head. "I'm guessing it wasn't the right thing to do?" Ella didn't meet her eyes when she asked this.

"No, I mean, it depends. I appreciate you wanting to stand up for me, but I can do it myself." Tiana felt a bit of pity for the woman who was so desperate to do the right thing but ended up being quite off track.

"But you didn't." Ella didn't pose it as a question. Just a matter-of-fact statement. She took a sip of her own iced drink now, her hand shaking very slightly.

"I didn't want to escalate him. Men like that"—Tiana let out a slow breath—"are volatile. You never know what could happen."

Ella nodded. "I had a whole script in my head, ready to go. Normally, I'm not good in situations like that. Thinking on my feet. But I was prepared."

"What were you going to say?" Tiana tilted her head to the side.

"I was going to tell him he was a shit-eating racist and they didn't serve what he eats here."

Tiana let out a loud belly laugh, and Ella looked rather satisfied with her response, sitting up in the chair proudly.

"Good, right?"

Tiana shook her head. "Definitely wouldn't have gone over well."

"You're probably right. But he deserved it."

"Yes, but my dad always said people eventually get what is coming to them. He'll get his someday." Tiana shrugged, and Ella nodded.

Tiana had thought a lot about that day since then. How Ella had tried to jump in to help but then she had noticed Tiana's hesitancy. She wondered if Ella felt like she needed to help Tiana, like Tiana couldn't help herself. But their friendship had come so naturally afterward. And each time Ella helped her, Tiana returned the favor tenfold. If she had been keeping track, she had gotten Ella out of far more binds than the other way around.

Now, Tiana pulled into Sammie's Motel, a look of disgust painted onto her face at the thought that Ella and the kids would sleep there. Ella had told her lots of stories about Sleezy Sammie, the owner. Apparently, he had always been gross. At least, that's what everyone in town said.

Ella was standing next to her silver SUV, and the moment they saw each other, they both began to cry.

9

Ella
April 25, 2022

While Ella thought herself a pretty competent problem-solver, Tiana was truly the fixer in their relationship. A bowling birthday party spoiled by the bowling alley flooding? Tiana either found a new set of lanes, or made it happen elsewhere, buying her own bowling pins and balls. A Halloween costume mishap? Tiana could sew up tears herself or locate a new costume altogether within a half hour. If she couldn't fix the problem, she would find somebody who could. So when Ella and the kids found themselves at a hotel that most certainly did not have bed bugs, it was all thanks to Tiana.

"Do you need anything else? Did you have something to eat?" Tiana set her purse down on the desk in the hotel room.

Ella shook her head, frowning. "I wasn't hungry. Neither were the kids when I asked." Ella had already changed into a pair of lounge clothes after spending far too long in her scrubs.

"You need to eat." Tiana didn't ask any more follow-up questions before pulling out her phone. After a moment of silence, she smiled. "Done. Pizza will be here in like 40 minutes."

"I really don't think I could eat right now."

"Let's see if you are still singing that tune when it arrives." Tiana knew that pizza was one of Ella's favorite guilty-pleasure dinners. It was cheap enough for a family of four, and something about it made her feel whole inside.

"You're right." Her voice sounded hollow as she stared at the door that led to the kids' conjoining room. She thought back to her conversation a few hours ago with Ryan. How she had told him they would just order pizza tonight. She hadn't been wrong. But everything else had gone horribly awry. Tiana planted herself on the edge of the bed next to Ella and rubbed her back in small, gentle circles.

"I know." The pair of them stared at the blank television screen, neither of them sure what to say.

"I just don't know who would have done it."

Tiana blinked at Ella's words. Throughout the chaos of arranging for a new hotel and trying to solicit a refund from Sleezy Sammie, they hadn't found time to discuss the day's events.

"It wasn't a heart attack?" Tiana continued to rub her back, her eyes glazing over a bit as she processed Ella's words.

Ella bit her bottom lip and shook her head. "They think it may have been a homicide." She pulled in a deep breath. "It must have been. There was so much blood."

"That or . . ." Tiana didn't finish her sentence because they both knew what word would come next: *suicide*.

"It looked like maybe there was a gunshot . . .," Ella reasoned. She hadn't thought to ask Clemens if their handgun was still in Ryan's nightstand. No matter how many times she tried, she couldn't bring herself to ask the kids what he looked like when they had found him. It felt like retraumatizing them. But at the same time, she knew the police would probably be doing that tomorrow.

"I don't think he would do that. I mean, there were no signs. Sometimes there are no signs, but usually, in those instances—" Tiana stopped herself. "Speculating isn't helpful, is it?"

"I'm not sure what would be helpful at this point. I wish I could talk to him. I just want to hear his voice." Ella's own voice cracked and tears began to fall down her cheeks. Tiana bit her bottom lip before standing up.

"Hold on a second."

Ella grabbed a tissue from the nightstand and violently blew her nose. After crying for half the evening, her sinuses were so congested she could already feel a migraine coming on.

Tiana returned to the bed with her phone in hand. There was a small glimmer in her brown eyes. Ella tucked her blonde hair behind her ears before fingering her earring on the right side. Small diamond studs, a gift from Ryan for their tenth anniversary.

"I don't know if this would be helpful, but it's something. If you don't want to, you don't have to." Tiana had pulled up the voicemails on her cell phone. Ella stared at the screen, particularly at Ryan's name.

"He gave me a call yesterday. I was with a client so I didn't answer, and I suppose what he talked about doesn't matter so much anymore." Tiana gently placed the phone in Ella's hand.

Knots twisted inside Ella's stomach, and she thought for a moment she might actually be sick. She had felt the same way in the bedroom earlier when she could smell the iron reek of blood. After a minute of contemplation, she brought herself to hit play.

"Hey, T. I should have figured you would be with somebody right now. But whatever. I was thinking about Ella's birthday coming up here soon. I know that 44 isn't a huge birthday or anything, but I just really want to do something special. She deserves so much, you know. Anyway, I'm rambling. Give me a call when you get a chance and we can talk. Or I can drop by. Just let me know. See ya."

Ella had been holding her breath for the entire call. She didn't realize it until she coughed and sputtered once the phone went silent.

"That doesn't sound like the plans of a man who is contemplating suicide." Tiana locked her phone and held it in her lap.

"No, it doesn't. Somebody did *this* to him."

Their eyes met for a moment, both of them obviously hurting from the realization. Who would want to hurt Ryan, one of the kindest and funniest men they knew? A man they both loved, albeit in very different ways.

"Any idea who?" Tiana asked, but Ella just shook her head.

"Not a clue."

10

Tiana
April 25, 2022

Once the Thomas family was fed (just as Tiana thought, they could not resist the smell of hot pizza) and tucked in for the night, she hopped back into her car to head home. Her brain felt foggy as she tried to process Ryan's death. None of it made sense. Ryan Thomas was not a man with enemies. In fact, Tiana could only imagine people disliking him for how damn charismatic he was.

There was a gnawing feeling in the pit of her stomach that this had nothing to do with Ryan at all. Her mind flicked through the other options as she sailed through a green light. Burglary gone wrong. Psychopath on a killing spree. Domestic—her brain stopped on that one. There was no way that Ella would ever have anything to do with her husband's death, despite all the statistics and stories she had heard over the years.

She put on her right turn signal and rubbed her right eye. Exhaustion was beginning to creep up on her. There was no point in contemplating murder when she was so tired, and when they had so little information. Tomorrow, once Ella was interviewed by the police, maybe she would know more. Tiana wasn't the praying type, but she glanced up at the night sky.

"If you're up there, please don't let it be awful. Please don't let this break them." She included the kids because she knew they were suffering, especially Sophia. She had always been a daddy's girl, and Tiana had seen children destroyed by much less.

"Let it be simple and done with." As she spoke, she wondered if she was just speaking awful things into existence. Normally, Ella would tell her that it would all be okay. That God was listening, and he had a plan. Tiana would have given her a small smile and said that the Devil had plans of his own. Then they would laugh. But she didn't think either of them would be laughing this time.

11

Ella
April 26, 2022

Ella had listened to podcast after podcast that detailed the incompetency of small-town police departments. That idea replayed in her mind as she stood with her kids at the reception desk. When she got dressed this morning, her black jeans felt rough against her skin. Even on the outside, she felt more fragile than usual.

"You said Thomas?" A woman sporting a name tag that said Geraldine sat at a desk, squinting at the computer screen. If her name wasn't enough to age her, the way she fumbled around on the computer, appearing to click aimlessly, indicated she was definitely ancient.

"Yes. I believe Clemens is the lead—" Ella stumbled over the word. Was he a detective? She couldn't remember if he had said so yesterday, but it only made sense. At least she hoped he was.

"Shit," Geraldine grumbled as she misclicked on the

computer, closing down their software entirely. "Let me just go get Dave." She pushed back her chair and pushed herself up with the help of the desk.

Ella glanced behind her at Nate and Sophia. Sophia's face was void of any emotion, but Ella could make out the annoyance in her eyes. Nate was on his phone, scrolling through something. Ella licked her lips and frowned.

"Do you think you guys can handle this?"

Nate looked at his mother now, and she wondered when he had grown so tall. She could see his ankles under the hem of his jeans, and she felt guilty for not noticing he needed a longer size sooner. Neither of her kids answered. Ella glanced down at her ballet flats, avoiding looking at them for the next part.

"Do you need a lawyer present?" Her question served a variety of purposes. Of course, she wanted to protect her kids, but she wanted to know if they felt they had anything to hide. They had found the body after all. Ella's mind replayed the image of Nate in front of the burning trash can. She wasn't sure if she knew her son all that well, and the past 24 hours had clouded that knowledge even more. A small slice of her brain, hidden deep, wondered why he was suddenly so compassionate and caring. Was it because they had all shared in a joint tragedy? Or was it something else?

"A lawyer?" Nate asked. "Aren't you supposed to always have a lawyer when you talk to the police?"

Her son wasn't wrong, but she had expected this comment to come from Sophia. She cataloged this response in the back of her mind and nodded.

"We don't have anything to hide," Sophia argued. "You'll be there, right, Mom?"

Ella gave a tight nod and turned back around just as

Dave Clemens appeared around the corner. She noticed now that he was balding in a rather unflattering manner—he had the appearance of a man in denial about his own hair loss. Ella couldn't decide if shaving his head bald was an option either. In Texas, it wasn't a good look for a white man to be completely bald without any facial hair. Actually, it wasn't a good look anywhere. The rest of him was well kept, apart from his larger belly. He was freshly shaved, wearing a powder-blue button-down and a navy tie. He had tan slacks on, and his shirt was remarkably stain-free. Ella decided he was not the type to eat a jelly donut anyway.

"Good morning." Dave had a file folder in his hand and did not reach out to shake Ella's. Her mind immediately judged him as acting hostile, even though that was an overreaction.

Ella cleared her throat before asking, "You have questions?"

Dave nodded. "Yes. I would like to speak to each of your children first."

Ella turned her head ever so slightly to see her children's faces, staring the hardest at Nate's. Her gaze was trying to penetrate his skull, to see if she should worry about what may be hiding there.

"Let's go then." Ella crossed her arms and nodded toward the hallway from which Dave had come. She knew that was where their interrogation rooms were from picking up Nate and Sophia yesterday.

Dave led them down the hallway, and Ella felt a shiver flow down her back like fingers across piano keys, hitting each vertebra in her spine.

"Which of you would like to go first?" He had stopped outside the same interrogation room from yesterday. Through the glass window, Ella could see the table already held several water bottles. A few chairs sat against the wall outside the room.

"I will." Sophia's voice was unwavering. Ella could make out a small glint in her eye and recognized it. Her daughter felt confident going into the interview. Determined.

"If you would please just take a seat right here, Nate." Dave gestured to a chair. Nate shrugged and sat down before he too stared at Sophia. "I'm sure you would like to join us, Mrs. Thomas."

Ella gave a tight nod as he opened the door and the pair made their way through.

The room felt several degrees warmer compared to the hallway, and the cool metal from the chair and table felt refreshing as Ella sat. Sophia perched on a chair and watched the door close.

The chair across from them scraped loudly as Clemens pulled it back and settled in it.

"You both seem like very intelligent women, but I want to make sure you are aware that this interview will be recorded. You are welcome to have a lawyer present or request one at any time. Understood?"

Ella tried not to flinch. Why was he insinuating her daughter needed a lawyer?

"Got it." Sophia's voice had a gruffness Ella hadn't heard before.

Clemens grabbed a water bottle and took a small sip. The silence in the room grew until Clemens began again.

"Sophia, I know you answered quite a few of my questions yesterday, but I want to go through it again."

Ella's mouth turned into a tight line. She hadn't known her children were questioned yesterday. For just a second, the room slanted as Ella became overwhelmed by the concept that there was so much she did not know.

"Yes." Sophia did not continue as Ella anticipated. Her daughter was smarter than she was at that age. Ella had always been naïve, but Sophia was educated, well-rounded. She knew not to carry on until a question was asked. Clemens looked slightly annoyed at her delay, but he brushed it off quickly.

"What time did you arrive home?"

"It was later than usual. There was a study session after school that I made Nate attend. He has state testing soon, and he needs to pass to graduate next year. We got home around four thirty."

Ella held her hands together in her lap to stop them from shaking. There had not been time last night to ask her children what they had discovered in their family home. Her mind drifted back to their house, how it had been marred by yesterday's events. She wasn't sure if she would even want to go back once they were done with the investigation. Ryan had died there. How was she supposed to sleep in that bed?

"What did you do when you arrived home?"

"I went upstairs to my bedroom. I noticed my parent's bedroom door was open, which was strange because they always keep it closed. Because of the cat." Sophia took a deep breath. "My dad was allergic. He didn't like the fur on the bed."

Ella winced when Sophia said *was*.

"Continue."

Ella did not like how cold Clemens's tone was, and she almost asked to end the interview there. Something told her that he was not on their side. But she didn't because she needed to know what happened next.

"I walked into the room, and my father was on the

bed. There was blood everywhere. I yelled for Nate." Sophia averted her eyes and stared at a corner of the room instead. Ella could see tears gathering in the corners of her daughter's eyes. "He came running up the stairs, and we both went to the bed. We checked for a pulse . . . but it was pretty obvious it was too late."

"You checked or Nate checked the body?"

Ella didn't like how Clemens said her son's name. She shifted in the chair and rubbed her hands on her black jeans. Her palms were sweating like she was the one being interrogated.

"We both did."

Ella turned her body slightly to get a better look at her daughter's face. She thought about her children's hands on their father's body. Bloody. Cold. Dead. She immediately felt very ill. Sophia's face now held something in it that Ella didn't recognize. She didn't think she had ever seen her daughter lie, but she thought that, just maybe, she was witnessing it for the first time.

12

Tiana
April 26, 2022

After canceling all her sessions for the day, Tiana found herself endlessly pacing her office, her brain envisioning the Thomas family in an interrogation room. Ella had told her that they needed to go, that otherwise it looked suspicious. Tiana felt differently. Life had taught her to inherently distrust cops.

After her feet had begun to ache from her pointy flats pinching her toes, she sat down behind her desk and did the only thing she could think of that might help. She called a lawyer.

* * *

Tiana trotted into the police station after Charlotte Reed—the only lawyer that Tiana knew. The instant Tiana watched Charlotte pull her black BMW into the police station parking lot, Tiana felt relief wash over her. She recognized the brand of clothing that Charlotte sported and smiled. Inside, she knew that it was wrong to make judgements based on someone's outward appearance, but she knew what it took to look as put together as Charlotte did.

"We discussed the retainer on the phone?" Charlotte stood a few inches taller than Tiana, but that was mostly from her heels. She clutched the handle of her briefcase—which looked more like a designer bag than something a 1950s businessman would have—in both hands in front of her.

"Yes." Tiana reached into her own purse, Kate Spade, and passed a check to Charlotte.

"Just so we are clear, I am not representing you. This is only meant to cover the Thomas family."

Tiana gave her a small nod, but fear nibbled on the corners of her mind. Would she need a lawyer? They had to be examining everyone close to the family. Tiana wondered if perhaps it was a bad idea to hire Charlotte. She was recently divorced from one of Ryan's coworkers, Samuel. Sam worked alongside Ryan for many years as real-estate agents. The Reeds had been present at many family barbecues and holiday parties.

Charlotte looked far different in this context than Tiana had ever seen her before. Normally, she was wearing sundresses or Lululemon activewear—still high end, but an entirely different vibe. When Sam and she had divorced, Sam got to keep custody of the friendship with the Thomas family while Charlotte got nearly everything else. Tiana told herself that Charlotte would never do anything that wasn't in the best interest of the children she had watched grow up, but she also knew that nobody was closer to the family than Tiana.

Charlotte was always just in the background.

"Let's not give them the chance to say something incriminating." Charlotte lifted her head high, her brown hair pulled in a tight, low ponytail trailing down her back. They made their way inside the station, and Tiana noticed how sweaty the back of her neck was.

"Morning, Geraldine," Charlotte sang out as she moved through the station without pausing.

Geraldine, the woman Tiana spotted behind the reception desk, only responded with a grimace. Even the air inside of the police station felt different to her— suffocating. Tiana hurried onward, nervous about what Ella would say. Ella was not thinking clearly in allowing her children to be interrogated without a lawyer. Tiana had not consulted her, but she figured she would want Ella to do the same for her. With Ryan gone, somebody had to step up to the plate. Tiana was more than willing for that to be her.

"Aunt T?" Nate sat up in the wooden chair and pushed his phone into the pocket of his hoodie. She recognized it as one she had bought him at a concert she had taken him to. Her heart shattered for a moment as she thought about how much she cared for this child and what he was going through.

"Hey." Tiana's voice broke, and she frowned. She wanted to appear strong for what was essentially her family, but she was on unsteady ground. She always considered herself to truly be their aunt. That she was like a second mother. But doubt crept in. What if Ella didn't see it that way? What if she was overstepping? What if their friendship didn't survive this tragedy?

"Hello, Nate." Charlotte held out a hand to Nate, a small smile on her lips. He looked mystified at her presence.

"Ms. Reed," Nate's mouth hung open for a moment, probably unsure whether that was even Charlotte's name anymore. Luckily for him, she had kept her ex-husband's last name since it was an integral part of her law practice.

"In the flesh. We'll chat more in a minute." Charlotte flashed a reassuring smile before turning around to open the door to the interrogation room. Tiana's eyes rose to the glass viewing window now, and she covered her hand with her mouth. Sophia's expression was hardened, and she was shaking her head. A few tears ran down Ella's face. Tiana wasn't sure if she wanted to hear what was being said so she knew or if she would rather never know.

The detective—Ella had said his name was Clemens—turned around and stood up as Charlotte announced her entrance in her grandiose manner. Tiana longed to have that amount of confidence, but she supposed it was all an act. A part of being a lawyer.

Ella looked up at the glass window, and while Tiana was pretty sure Ella couldn't see her, she thought her friend knew she was there. The smallest smile appeared on Ella's lips, and Tiana let go of a breath she hadn't known she was holding.

13

Ella
April 26, 2022

When Clemens had pulled out the first of the crime-scene photographs, Ella knew her children were being set up for something. How these people could ever imagine that her children would be the ones to murder their own father, she didn't know. Then Charlotte had walked in, and Ella felt like she had just been rescued from an oncoming tsunami. Now, Ella stood outside the interview room, watching intently, while Tiana paced behind her.

"I swear to God, if you don't stop moving, I will kill you." As the words tumbled out of her mouth, Ella flinched.

Nate's head jerked up, and Tiana stopped in her tracks. The two women stared at each other for a few seconds before breaking into nervous laughter. A smile crept onto Nate's lips, and Ella let out a deep breath once the giggle subsided.

"Was there anybody else in the home? Did you see someone run away from the house maybe?" Clemens asked. Sophia shook her head. Charlotte put a gentle hand on Sophia's arm.

"You need to respond verbally for the recording."

"No." Sophia's eyes had grown darker by the moment. Ella knew that her daughter was strong, but she wondered what it would take to topple her.

"Did you see anything suspicious? Anything out of the ordinary? Even that morning?"

"You mean other than my father's blood splattered all over the walls of our home? No."

Ella looked away from the intensity of Sophia's eyes, and Tiana put a hand on her shoulder.

"It's okay. She's holding her own. Charlotte will make sure he doesn't go too far."

Ella wanted to tell her that he already had, but she didn't.

"Charlotte," Ella began, letting out a slow breath. She didn't know how much a lawyer like her would cost, but she knew that Charlotte wouldn't be doing this for free. They were never that close.

"She's taken care of."

Tears blurred Ella's vision for a moment, and she blinked to clear them. "Thank you."

Tiana shook her head. "Don't give it a moment's thought." Her friend reached down and took Ella's hand in her own. "It's all going to be okay. They'll find who did this."

Ella resisted the urge to roll her eyes. The cops were sitting around traumatizing her children instead of looking for who had hurt her family. She didn't feel confident in their skills. She also didn't want to attack Tiana for trying to be comforting, so she said nothing.

Everyone in the interview room was standing now, and Charlotte guided Sophia out of the room.

"Nate." Clemens cleared his throat and gestured toward the room. Ella felt her throat tighten with each breath, like the tightening of a screw. Sophia plopped down in the chair next to the one Nate vacated as he made his way into the room. He threw a sideways glance at Ella, appearing to offer a reassuring smile. But it was the same smile he always used whenever he got himself mixed up in trouble. While the corners of his mouth were upturned, there was a sadness in his brown eyes. This time, they looked a bit filled with fear too.

Ella pulled her hand away from Tiana's, rubbing her palms together until they felt hot from friction.

"This isn't good," Ella whispered after the door had shut. This time, Tiana didn't offer any comfort.

* * *

Clemens ran through the same questions with Nate, whose responses mirrored Sophia's perfectly. Ella's nerves were finally starting to calm by the time his interview wrapped up. When Clemens walked out of the room, Ella was ready to leave the station. She wanted nothing more than to ignore the world and partake in a coma-like sleep in her own bed. But when she envisioned her bedroom, the walls splattered with blood, the desire twisted her stomach. She was pretty sure their house still wouldn't be available for them anyway.

"Mrs. Thomas," Clemens called, pulling Ella out of her daydream. She turned, oversized black sunglasses in her hand, ready to leave, only to see Clemens gesturing to the interview room.

"Does this need to happen now?" Charlotte asked indignantly. Once again, Ella said a silent thank you to Tiana for bringing a lawyer. She wasn't sure why she hadn't decided to do it herself. Maybe it was the money. Maybe it was the false sense that her family didn't do anything wrong and didn't need one. It was a reckless decision, and Ella admonished herself for a moment. Ryan had always been the one to make clearcut decisions, but she needed to step up for her kids. But at the end of the day, Tiana had been the one to call the lawyer, and maybe Tiana was all they really needed.

"Just five minutes. All I need."

Charlotte rolled her eyes. "Fine, but I am setting a timer."

Ella gave a small nod and moved toward the room, with Charlotte close behind her. When they were all settled into the metal chairs, Ella with her purse perched on her lap and one arm wrapped around it like the bag was a child's stuffed animal, Clemens began.

"I know these questions will be uncomfortable, but they are crucial to our investigation."

Her eyes darted to the mirror behind Clemens's head where her children were concealed. The last thing she wanted was for them to hear something unsavory about their father, but she forced the fear away because she couldn't imagine Ryan doing anything that the kids couldn't hear about. A fog had settled over her brain, making its way into every wrinkle and crevice. She couldn't decide if she was overreacting, but maybe she wasn't doing enough. She swallowed hard.

"I understand." She forced her voice to be strong, because otherwise, she was afraid nobody would be able to hear her.

"How were things financially? Were you in any trouble?"

"Things were tight." She swallowed hard and remembered the kids were out of sight. Both she and Ryan had reasonable life insurance policies, so the last thing she wanted was for her children to worry. "But we always got by fine." Ella forced a tight smile on her lips.

"Was Ryan involved with anybody?" Clemens asked, not once looking down at the folder before him. Ella's mind filled with images of Tony Soprano. She shook her head immediately; imagining if her husband's killing was related to some kind of mob or gang seemed ridiculous. But Clemens pushed forward. "Romantically?"

Ella's breath caught in her throat, and she hoped that nobody else in the room heard it, but a small glimmer in Clemens's eyes told her that he had.

"I have no reason to suspect that my husband was cheating."

But every married woman's greatest fear is her husband cheating, Ella thought. They had been married for almost twenty years. Her mind went back to the room outside, to her children and her best friend listening. And for just a small second, she wondered just how close her best friend had been with her husband. The thought was fleeting as her mind wandered back to Ryan's voicemail.

14

Tiana
April 26, 2022

"Detective, do you have any real questions?" Charlotte's forceful voice nearly made Tiana flinch. She wondered if Charlotte did that because she was so used to men trying to ignore her while she was working. Clemens grumbled something Tiana couldn't quite make out. "Anything based on evidence, Dave?"

Clemens just shook his head.

"Let's go, Ella."

Tiana examined her best friend's face as she rose out of the chair. Ella looked as if she hadn't heard a word said, and her eyes wandered around the room almost as if she was on drugs. Tiana shook her head immediately. There was no way Ella of all people would be on drugs, particularly when her children needed her more than ever. But there was something in her eyes that Tiana couldn't read, and it scared her.

* * *

"Do you think any of those things the detective said are really possible?" Ella asked as they sat at the same small-town coffee shop they had met at years before. Sophia and Nate were back at the hotel—they hadn't wanted to spend more time out and about town. Their community was small enough that they would likely see someone they knew, but Ella had told Tiana she couldn't stand to spend another moment in the hotel.

"What things?" Tiana tried to meet Ella's eyes, but they were staring out the large coffee shop windows at the cars driving past.

"Cheating?" Ella's eyes flicked back to Tiana, and Tiana frowned in response.

"No, of course not. Ryan was head over heels for you. You heard that voicemail."

Ella nodded and took a sip of her latte, appearing satisfied.

"If I knew any differently, I would tell you." Tiana let out a slow breath. "I was thinking about Nate and Sophia. You might want to get them into some therapy sooner rather than later. Seeing Ryan like that is a huge source of trauma. I can give you some names."

Tiana's face fell as she saw Ella's eyes cloud over. She knew without asking what she was thinking.

"I'm sure one of them takes your insurance."

"They probably do." Ella gave a tight nod. "But we don't really have extra money for co-pays right now. And I don't think the life insurance policy is going to be showing up any time soon, considering Clemens thinks I killed him."

"What?" Tiana shook her head, setting her iced coffee down on the scarred wooden table. She crossed her arms, growing more uneasy by the second. "He didn't say that."

"He didn't have to. You know that's the first person they would suspect."

Tiana's stomach felt like it was being pulled inside out. She had to admit Ella was right, but nobody could really believe that was what happened. Ella had no motive whatsoever. Tiana gave a small shrug because she couldn't bring herself to speak.

"Can you do it?" Ella was back to staring out the window.

"Do what?" Tiana's palms felt sweaty. She couldn't be talking about killing Ryan, but she thought back to how Ella had said money was tight. Maybe they needed the life insurance more than she thought. If she had to decide between caring for her family and killing her husband, what would she choose? Tiana tried to push the intrusive thoughts away.

"Do therapy with the kids."

At the same time that Tiana felt relief that her best friend wasn't asking her if she was capable of murder, she could feel her throat tighten.

"That's really a conflict of interest, Ella. I don't think I am the best option. If you need money to—"

"I cannot take more money from you." Ella's eyes were set on Tiana's face now, and she wondered for just a second if Ryan's death would be the thing that would bring down their friendship after so many years. "The kids trust you. They'll talk to you."

Tiana felt like her chest was caving in, crushing into vital organs, and she tried to force out some small breaths, but her windpipe felt jagged.

"You're right."

Ella took a sip of her latte and nodded. "Can you start tomorrow?"

15

Ella
April 26, 2022

"We don't need therapy!" Sophia argued, pacing across her mother's hotel room.

"Sophia," Ella sighed, shaking her head. The argument had been going on for 10 minutes already, and she was getting nowhere.

"Don't say my name like that!"

Ella pulled in a slow breath. "I care about you, and I know you may not be interested right now, but I think it will really help you down the road."

"Jesus Christ. If you cared about me, you would listen!" Sophia tossed her hands up and stopped at the window, staring down at the air conditioner. Her dirty blonde hair blew backwards with the cool air, and Ella imagined her at the beach, feeling the salty breeze. Her heart crumbled at the thought that they would never have another beach vacation with Ryan. They hadn't gone often, but they always made a point to go every other year when they could afford it. Her favorite memories were at North Beach, building sandcastles with the kids or watching the sunset with Ryan. Things had changed since Nate and Sophia had gotten older. The trips weren't the same as when they were little, and they never could be now that Ryan couldn't come.

"North Beach," Ella murmured. Sophia snapped around.

"What?"

"We should scatter his ashes there."

A horrified expression fell upon Sophia's face, her skin turning pale.

"Ashes . . ." Sophia swallowed and sat down on the bed next to her mother's, staring at the ugly floral comforter. "He's being cremated?"

"That is what he wanted. I mean, at least I think so. We never did sit down and outline everything. But they can't do anything until the autopsy is done."

Silence fell over the room like an avalanche, icing their veins as it fell.

Sophia couldn't look up at her mother. Ella wondered if Nate was listening next door, or if he had headphones in listening to some death metal. It occurred to her that she didn't even know if that was the music he listened to nowadays. Tiana had taken him to a concert a little while ago, but Ella couldn't remember the genre.

"Do you think they already started?"

"What?" Ella asked, her face softening now. Her daughter was coming back to her piece by piece. She knew that the shock of Ryan's death had just thrown her briefly off course.

"The autopsy." Tears were welling in her eyes, and her face was becoming red, just like it did before she cried as a baby. "Do you think that Dad's lying cut open in some cold room right this minute?"

Goosebumps crawled across Ella's neck. She tried to imagine what Sophia was seeing in her mind: Her beloved father spliced open, his heart exposed to the open air. But then, Ella remembered the blood in their bedroom. Sophia wasn't envisioning a clean body like Ella was. Sophia was imagining what she had seen in the bedroom when she realized her father was dead.

Ella rose and moved next to her daughter, wrapping an arm around her tightly, pulling her as close as she could. Sophia didn't resist and curled into her mother's body. The two of them cried together without speaking until finally, Sophia pulled away and her eyes regarded her mother sharply.

"I'll go to therapy."

Ella let out a slow breath and gave her daughter a sad smile. She couldn't even begin to imagine the mess the past 24 hours had created in her daughter's mind. She just hoped that Tiana would be able to clean it all up.

16

Tiana
April 27, 2022

When Tiana finally woke up, after finally giving in and taking a Xanax at two in the morning, she felt like her nerves were live wires. A pit had been growing larger and larger inside her stomach ever since Ella had asked her to do a few sessions with Nate and Sophia. Originally, Tiana had wanted to start with Sophia, but Ella had said she was a bit resistant, so they decided Nate should take the first appointment.

Tiana was putting the finishing touches on her hair when she heard Nate open the front door downstairs. Ollie's nails clacked against the hardwood floor as he rushed to greet him, and Tiana made a mental note to trim them later on.

"Be right there!" she called down the stairs, adjusting her black dress shirt to tuck into her red pants. The entire morning she had felt something equivalent to getting ready for a first date. While she found that emotion disturbing, she decided not to fixate on it too much. Tiana trotted down the stairs, expecting to see Nate perched in the office, but it was empty. Confusion bloomed on her face as she moved toward the kitchen, the only other open space on the first floor.

Nate was perched on one of the wooden kitchen chairs, leaning forward and holding Ollie against himself. Ollie held his head against Nate's face. She had always known Ollie would make a great therapy dog, though she had never tested out that theory. Under different circumstances, Tiana would have pulled out her phone and snapped a quick picture. It could even end up being her lock-screen photo. But it wasn't that kind of moment.

"Hey, Nate." Tiana was surprised when her voice didn't break. She felt whiplash from envisioning all the other times he had been in her kitchen. He and Sophia baking Christmas cookies every year. The tradition had evolved over the years, with them making gingerbread men with various forms of amputated limbs, including one particularly unfortunate soul which had been decapitated. Nate's idea, of course.

"Hi, Aunt T." His voice was muffled by Ollie's body. Tiana slowly crossed the kitchen, moving to the four-person glass dining table. Instinctually, her arms wrapped around him, enveloping both Nate's scrawny shoulders and Ollie's tank of a body. Ollie's tail whipped around, smashing into Tiana's legs, and she let out a small laugh. Ollie was exhilarated by this reaction and wrenched himself away from their grasp, spinning in a circle, battering them both with his skinny gray tail.

"Ouch!" Nate laughed out, trying to pull away, but there was no way in hell Tiana was letting him go. "Ollie, please, no!" Nate was bent over far enough that the dog's whip was flicking into Nate's face, and Tiana let out a deep belly laugh. Nate's laughter echoed hers as they both pulled away, and Ollie stared between the both of them, wondering what he could have possibly done to make the pair pull apart. He settled down on his hind leg just for a moment before lying down on the cool hardwood floor, his tongue swiping a small section of the floor while he panted.

The laughter slowly died out until Tiana watched Nate look away from her, avoiding eye contact. She cleared her throat, trying to figure out how they were going to process anything he was going to say today. Her gut told her to change her mind, say no, and find someone else to treat the children that were the closest thing she had ever had to offspring. But Tiana thought back to the fragility she had felt yesterday when speaking to Ella, and a deep fear nagged at the back of her mind that if she didn't do this, the friendship would be over, and she would lose more than she was willing to.

"Should we sit down in the office?" Tiana asked, reaching into the refrigerator, trying to act casual as she pulled out a water for herself and a can of Monster for Nate. She personally hated the stuff, but he loved it, and she couldn't help but humor him at least occasionally. And this seemed like more than a worthy occasion.

"Can't we stay in here?" His voice cracked as he asked the question. Tiana shook her head immediately, her hair bouncing around her face.

"Absolutely not. This is weird enough as it is. I'm drawing a boundary."

Nate rolled his eyes and rose to his feet. Tiana's eyes glanced at his black Converses, noticing the mud dried to the bottom edges.

"You better not be tracking that in here," she warned but cringed when she realized how motherly she sounded.

"It's from the rain the other day. I didn't get a chance to clean them before . . ."

Tiana handed him the energy drink and took a sip of her own water, forcing herself to swallow down her guilt.

"I could have driven you home. It wasn't a problem."

"I know. We just didn't know when we were going to get out of that study session. I tried to bail early, but Sophia—" He shrugged in a way that finished the sentence for him. Sophia could be a firecracker when she wanted to be, and her personality ruled over those around her.

Tiana gave a tight nod as she moved into her former living room, settling into her normal leather armchair, watching as Ollie waited by the doorway, skeptical about whether he was permitted inside. Normally, he was crated upstairs during all her sessions, but she couldn't see why he needed to be today. She smiled and he came rushing forward, joy obvious on his face.

Nate patted the couch, inviting him up. Tiana opened her mouth to stop him, thinking of long scratches across the leather, but she stopped short. Ollie might make Nate more comfortable, let him open up more. She closed her mouth and crossed her right leg over her left, pulling her black blouse away from her stomach, and let out a slow breath.

"Where do you want to start?"

Nate shrugged, already clamming up after the moment of vulnerability in the kitchen.

"How about we leave the hard stuff aside for now? We can talk about that day later. Let's talk about now. How are you feeling?" Tiana was surprised how easily she slipped back into the role of a therapist. Her mind had already created a block between herself and the patient.

Nate cracked open the drink. Tiana's imagination told her she could smell the sickly-sweet liquid from here, and one of her back molars surged with a quick flash of pain. Her eyes shifted to the geometric area rug as her mind wandered just for a brief moment, wondering if somebody could experience PTSD from a root canal.

"Empty."

Tiana blinked, glancing back at his drink, thinking he had chugged the entire thing while she was distracted.

"What?" She squinted and rubbed her hand down her blouse, flattening it despite having just pulled it out to be more comfortable.

"Empty. I'm feeling empty."

Tiana swallowed hard, feeling blood drain out of her face. All she could think about was how bad of an idea this was.

17

Ella
April 27, 2022

A loud knock on the hotel-room door startled Ella, pulling her out of a downward spiral. She glanced at her smart watch. How long had she been staring at the red hotel-room curtains? It had been at least an hour since she had given Nate the keys to her car to go to Tiana's, and roughly 45 minutes since Charlotte had texted saying she needed to come by to 'talk.' Ella's last thought before she disassociated while staring at the curtains was that Charlotte was going to refuse her as a client. There was too much history there, and they hadn't exactly been friendly since she divorced Sam.

After the second forceful knock, Ella decided she had no choice but to let Charlotte in to cut ties with the train wreck that was her life. She absent-mindedly peeked through the peephole, then let Charlotte in.

She was dressed in a navy pantsuit with beige heels, and Ella would be lying if she said she wasn't envious of her style and body. Ella had gained a few extra pounds with each pregnancy, and while she wouldn't exactly say she had let herself go, she hadn't put in an effort to stay fit like Ryan had. She could imagine him whispering in her ear now, knowing exactly what she was thinking when she saw Charlotte, and telling her he wouldn't trade her for anything in the world. His love had been one of the reasons she never worried about losing any weight. There were too many memories to be made to spend time counting calories or sweating on an elliptical.

"How are you holding up?" Charlotte asked as she sat down on the office chair and spun around to face Ella.

Ella swallowed hard, and though a small part of her mind was negative, she told herself that Charlotte wasn't the type to make small talk before cutting off a client. To Charlotte, it would have been a waste of time and money.

"I'm not sure how to answer that question."

Ella wondered how people with cancer felt when they were asked the same thing. Knowing that their future might be doomed, they might try to hold onto hope and feel optimistic. They might put on a brave face for everyone else. But the tragedy of Ella's life had already occurred. There wasn't any time to prepare. To get into the right mindset. It was like being flung from a vehicle, knowing you were going to splatter on the pavement only to be pried up with a shovel, but the impact never came. You just keep hurtling through the air already filled with dread.

"I'm not sure why I even asked." Charlotte rested her hands in her lap, looking down at her feet. A brief silence passed before she cleared her throat and began speaking again. "I'm sure you want to know why I'm here."

Ella gave a tight nod but didn't bother speaking. Words felt dangerous—she could break into tears at any moment, but she had quickly learned if she didn't say anything, tears were harder to come by.

"The detectives have asked us to put together a list of people who may have been in your home in the past six months, particularly in your bedroom." Charlotte had lifted her eyes to stare directly at Ella, and she couldn't shake the feeling Charlotte was trying to get a reaction.

"Why?" Ella's voice came out louder than she intended, and she mouthed *sorry* after, without really meaning it.

"That's the exact right question." Charlotte paused, seeming to carefully contemplate what she said next. "Usually, it means they have found some piece of evidence that doesn't fit. They already have hair samples and fingerprints from everyone in the family. Those are easy to collect—but when they find something out of the ordinary, they ask for a list."

"Does this mean they have a lead?" Ella's chest felt hollow and light at the same time. Maybe they didn't think it was her any longer—maybe they had found evidence someone else had been there.

"Not necessarily. Ella, I hate to ask this, but was Ryan having an affair? Did you have any suspicions that he might be—"

"No." Ella had wanted her voice to be forceful this time, but instead, it came out feeble. Her body kept working against her.

"There is nothing that sticks out to you that could be a red flag?" Charlotte's voice was strong and steady, which Ella envied. She sounded just like she had in the police station: confident. Ella just wished her lawyer wasn't so confident her husband was having an affair.

Ella cleared her throat this time before speaking. "No red flags." She didn't feel entirely sure though. Ryan worked nights. He was at dinner parties, a lot. He had kept in great shape even as they entered their forties.

Charlotte nodded and seemed to believe her despite her own personal insights.

"If there is no affair, then it is likely they found evidence that could be from a murderer. But if they think it was evidence from an affair, that will give them even more reason to suspect you."

Silence was heavy in the room as the sound of Ella's own heart racing swelled in her ears. Charlotte appeared to be growing more uncomfortable as each second ticked by.

"They say, 'hell hath no fury like a woman scorned.' Cops eat that shit up," Charlotte rambled. "My theory is they are so angry at all the women that had ever rejected them that they can't help but blame a woman. It's like they are the most socially acceptable version of an incel."

Sophia had told her that term once, and all Ella could think about was all the white, male shooters at schools and malls. Based on the news the past few years, cops really didn't seem that far off.

"Anyway, we can choose to cooperate and offer them a list or not. My recommendation is we comply if you feel positive there was no affair. But like I said: a single red flag, we shouldn't comply. Let them do the work themselves."

"Give them nothing," Ella whispered, pulling in a

deep breath. She thought of how Clemens had interrogated her children, pulling out crime-scene photos, traumatizing them all over again. "Those assholes deserve nothing."

18

Tiana
April 27, 2022

"Should I even be talking to you about all this?" Nate asked, shifting uncomfortably on the couch, moving Ollie's elbow off his thigh.

"You can talk about anything you want to. It's therapy." Tiana wanted to lie; she wanted to tell him to be very selective about what he shared because she didn't want to have to hide too much from Ella. More than that, she really didn't want him to share anything that may lurk inside her head as she tried to fall asleep at night.

"Can we talk about your dad?" Nate asked, his eyes softening a bit. It was weird to think that there were huge parts of her own life that Nate didn't know about. Her and Ella's friendship had not yet begun when Tiana's father passed away. If they had been friends, Nate would have only been seven. Over the years, she was sure she had mentioned her father, only in passing, but neither of the kids had ever asked for a deep dive into her childhood.

"If that's what you want."

"I think it would make me feel better. He's been gone for a long time, and I think it would just be helpful to—" Nate cleared his throat, trying to dodge tears. "To hear from someone who is further away from it."

"His name was Jeremiah Hill, but everybody he ever knew called him Jerry. Or Mr. Hill. He was a social studies teacher for most of his life, and he was good at it. But I guess I'm a little biased. The thing he loved the most was being around people. That was his happy place."

Now Tiana was trying to avoid tears. She had loved her father so much, although it could never compare to how much he loved her.

"How did he die?" Nate was watching her carefully now, his breathing jagged. Tiana's instincts told her maybe they should stop. It was too traumatic—he was clearly distressed, but she decided that was just a lie she was telling herself. In reality, he was pushing the conversation on.

"He had a heart attack. He was in his home"—Tiana contemplated finishing the sentence for a second—"alone. He was by himself." Now that she had started, she couldn't stop the words from tumbling out. "His neighbor found him. They used to get coffee at McDonald's together every morning. There was a group of like six guys. They went there because they could get a 10 percent discount on a dollar coffee. I always thought that was funny. Ten cents off was enough to bring the senior citizens in droves." Tiana let out a small sigh, the corner of her mouth slightly upturned.

"Anyway, he had a heart attack in the living room and his neighbor found him. He was the one who called me." A single tear slid down her cheek.

Nate nodded and pet Ollie without looking at him. Tiana fought the urge to get up and pull her dog up against herself for comfort, but that seemed inappropriate considering she was the adult here—not to mention, the therapist.

"How long was he there?"

Nate's words caught her off guard. She blinked, discomfort blooming in her chest. She felt chills roll down her back, and she forced herself to sit up a bit straighter.

"A little over a day."

Nate nodded as if he was following the beat to his own song. Tiana ran her tongue over her lips, realizing how dry her mouth felt.

"I guess things could have been worse then."

"With your dad?" Tiana asked, her voice cracking.

"Yeah. At least it was"—Nate contemplated for a moment—"recent, I guess."

Tiana imagined her true-crime shows with insensitive cops saying they had a fresh corpse. She wondered if that was what Nate originally meant to say.

"Sophia asked my mom last night if she thought they were doing the autopsy already."

Tiana's face looked grim, but she nodded.

"I've been thinking about that a lot."

"The autopsy?" Tiana asked, fidgeting in her seat.

"His body. How he looked—" Nate showed no signs of tears now. He stared across the room into the distance.

The front doorbell buzzed loudly, startling both Tiana and Nate. Ollie hauled himself off the couch and let out a single bark. Tiana glanced at her watch. They had gone over by about ten minutes. Nate rose from the couch without any prompting.

"I'll catch you later, Aunt T." He moved toward her and gave her a loose hug while she remained glued to the armchair.

"Love you," she muttered, trying to blink away the negative thoughts that had wormed their way into her mind. She could hear him close the door to her office and open the front.

"She said to tell you she'll be ready in a minute."

"Okay, thank you."

Tiana imagined the two of them standing in the crowded foyer.

"Have a nice day," Nate called. The front door closed gently behind him.

Tiana reached up and touched her cheeks, her fingers coming away wet with tears. She loved Nate. She would never think he could hurt a fly. But a tiny voice in the back of her mind told her maybe he could.

19

Ella
April 27, 2022

"When can we go home?" Sophia asked, stuffing a french fry into her mouth. They had picked up food from the diner just down the street. Initially, they had planned on eating there, but word was spreading around town quickly, and Ella couldn't handle being stared at.

"Charlotte said they are combing the scene still." Ella wiped some ranch dressing from the corner of her mouth. To her, there was nothing as good as a salad with all the fixings and coated in homemade ranch.

"They're trying to find evidence to prove we did it," Nate murmured from the armchair in the corner.

Sophia spun around in the desk chair to look at him, her mouth falling open, partially chewed fries visible from where Ella sat on the bed.

"What the hell is wrong with you? Mom, are you just going to let him say stuff like that?"

Ella took another bite of her salad to give her a second to figure out her answer. Sophia's eyes were filled with rage, and Ella couldn't very well let her son go around suggesting they could at all be responsible, even if that's not what he meant.

"Nate, for the time being, it's probably better we don't make comments like that."

"But it's true, right? Who are their main suspects? Us." Nate's voice was soft, filled with sadness, not anger. Ella tried to shake the feeling that he thought they deserved the attention.

"But we are all innocent. We have nothing to worry about."

The trio fell silent; none of them had anything more to say on the topic. The news coverage on the TV shifted from a bad traffic accident to a missing woman. They showed a large photo of her, red curls falling perfectly around her face. Ella forced herself to listen to the story, but trying to focus on anything proved difficult these days.

"Kelly Carter was last seen on Monday. Police encourage anyone with information about Kelly's whereabouts to call their tip line at—" Ella blinked, staring at the woman's photograph. She was gorgeous: long curly red hair, pale skin with a spattering of freckles, and a sharp jawline. The TV was now showing a short clip from a press conference. Mr. and Mrs. Carter stood at a podium, him asking for Kelly's safe return while Mrs. Carter cried beside him. Her chest felt like it had been scraped out—but as she glanced between Nate and Sophia, who were exchanging pointed looks, clearly still debating Nate's suspect comments, she felt the smallest bit grateful she had lost Ryan and not one of them.

Ella thought back to the days when Nate and Sophia were both too young for school. Ryan and she had decided she would be a stay-at-home mom since childcare was ridiculously expensive and she hadn't yet gone back to school to earn her associate's degree, so her earning potential was limited, to say the least. That was just before the housing market crashed and Ryan was making good money as a realtor, even without working ridiculous hours.

Regardless, her favorite memories were when Ryan would have to work late, so she would have the kids to herself. Instead of cooking, they would order a pizza (always just cheese—the kids were picky and Ella didn't mind) and cuddle up on the large brown couch in the living room. With only the TV lighting up the room, they would rewatch Disney movies the kids had already seen a thousand times. Nate would usually fall asleep before the movie was over, and it would be just her and Sophia, Nate looking utterly serene for once as a child. He was always all over the walls while Sophia was the girl who Ella had to remind herself to check on: since she was so quiet, she blended in easily. It was awful to admit, but Ella liked Nate the best when he was asleep.

Now the pair of them were throwing invisible knives across the room, and despite feeling overwhelmed by the fact that she was now a single mother, she thought things might just be okay. Her kids cared about each other enough to argue (without physically hurting each other), and they were going to stick together through all this. She was sure of it.

20

Tiana
April 27, 2022

That night, Tiana's thumb had hovered over the call button to reach out to Ella so many times. They had kept in touch through texts, but they hadn't actually spoken since the coffee shop. Tiana's mind was playing a nonstop game of tug-of-war, trying to decide if or what she could tell Ella without jeopardizing her license. Eventually, she decided not to call because what would she say? *"Nate was throwing out really weird vibes in therapy today and I have a vague feeling he might be responsible"*—she couldn't even let herself finish that thought. Nate had always trusted her, and he shared things with her he didn't trust other adults with.

Just as her mind had nearly arrived at a total mental breakdown from overthinking Nate's words, she forced herself to repeat aloud that "all people process grief differently" until her hands felt less clammy.

Tiana sat down at her desk to digitize her patient notes for the day, leaving Nate's for last. It had been a relatively easy day: mostly maintenance appointments with long-standing clients who were doing well. But Nate's notes felt complicated. The cursor blinked in front of Tiana, and she felt her throat tighten.

"Oh, Nate." She took a small sip of the white wine she had been nursing for the last hour, finding herself wanting the drink for comfort but not really enjoying it. With her slender fingers perched above the keyboard, she made a decision. If Nate had done something, it wouldn't be long before they turned their attention to her as his therapist. It wouldn't take much for the police to subpoena the records from their sessions. Really, the question Tiana had been struggling with all day was what would she do if she found out the truth and it wasn't what she wanted to hear. With her fingers now moving swiftly along the keyboard, she made a commitment.

"I'll keep you safe." The sound of her own voice surprised her. You didn't need to be somebody's mother to protect them. And no matter what Nate told her, the cops would never read about it. It was the nicest thing she could do for Nate, for Ella, and honestly, for herself.

21

Ella
April 28, 2022

"I'm coming to pick you up right now."

Ella sat up in bed, Charlotte's words playing pinball inside her skull. "What, why?"

"The police called. They want you in for questioning. They must have found something."

Ella swallowed hard and forced her body onto her feet and toward her suitcase. Nothing said unhinged like wearing pajamas to a police interview. She dug around, searching for something that could at least pass as athleisure.

"What is it?"

"I reached out to all my usual contacts, and they had no idea. Looks like they are keeping this one close to the vest." Charlotte's voice sounded flustered, and Ella wondered if she was actually worried about the case. Ella had never been in trouble before, but she knew your lawyer being worried was not a good sign.

Ella hung up with Charlotte and changed in the bathroom. She moved into the doorframe of the conjoining room. Nate was lying down on the bed, scrolling through some kind of social media. For a brief second, she wondered if Nate was reading news articles about Ryan, but she told herself he wouldn't waste time doing a thing like that. Not when there were so many more entertaining things to look at on the internet. Especially as a teenage boy.

"I need to go into the police station. Since Sophia has the car, do you want to stay here and wait for her or come with me and Charlotte?"

After a few seconds, Nate's eyes flicked up to her.

"Sorry, can you say that again?"

Nate had the same horrible habit as Ryan: They were never listening until you made sure you had their full attention. Ella had repeated herself so much over the course of her marriage that she had gotten into the habit of calling Ryan's name before she went into any detail. She frowned at the memory.

"Charlotte's taking me to the station. Do you want to come or wait here for your sister?"

Nate looked up at the ceiling, bopping his head from side to side as he contemplated. "I'll wait. I don't really want to see that asshat cop again anyway."

Ella suppressed the urge to admonish her seventeen-year-old son for swearing because a part of her felt proud for him calling Clemens what he was.

"No problem. Can you send me a text when Sophia gets back?"

Nate nodded and rolled over so his back was facing Ella.

"Love you," she called, but he had already slipped earbuds in. She grabbed her purse and checked her blonde hair before heading out the door, feeling hopeful the police had a lead that would pull attention away from herself.

22

Tiana
April 28, 2022

"What did Nate tell you when you two talked?" Sophia asked, her legs folded under her petite body as she perched on Tiana's couch. She clutched a forest-green throw pillow against her chest, something Tiana had made a mental note of.

"You know I can't discuss what he told me. Did you ask him yourself?" Tiana forced an encouraging smile, but it disappeared quickly when she realized how fake it felt. Until she had met with Sophia, she had never realized how much of being a therapist was acting. She spent a lot of time concealing her own emotions or pretending to be encouraging or supportive even when she didn't agree with a patient.

"Of course, I did. But he won't really talk to me since this all happened." Sophia's eyes moved all around the room, settling on many places but never on Tiana.

"Why do you think that is?" Tiana uncrossed her legs and leaned forward in her chair, her blush top swaying with the movement. She rested her elbows on her knees, hoping to get Sophia to look at her.

"I think he's mad that I made him go to the study session. Maybe if we had just gotten home sooner—" Her voice cracked and tears began falling instantly.

Tiana instinctively reached to the coffee table and held out the tissues for Sophia. She frantically grabbed several tissues, wadding a few up into a ball for her to blow her nose.

Neither of them spoke as Sophia cried and sniffled for a full minute. Eventually, she pulled herself together enough to speak.

"I know if we got there sooner, maybe we could have done more, but we didn't. I can't help what has already happened."

"Of course, you can't. We all handle these things very differently, and Nate is struggling just like you are. I do wonder though . . ." Tiana leaned forward again, trying to get a better look at Sophia's face, which was angled away from her, staring out the front window. "Do you blame yourself?"

"What?" Sophia's eyes flashed back to Tiana.

Confusion bloomed on Tiana's face. "I mean, do you blame yourself for not getting there sooner?"

Sophia let out a dry laugh. "Oh. I guess, maybe."

Tiana frowned, trying to figure out why Sophia would even think for a second that she was accusing her of her father's murder.

"Sophia, I am very concerned about you. You need to know that there was nothing you could have done to stop your father from being killed. Nothing. I know it is easy to run through scenarios in your head, but that is not healthy. You would never tell a woman who was raped that maybe she shouldn't have gone out that night. It is not your fault."

Sophia gave a tight nod, but Tiana didn't feel satisfied.

"I've never even seen you hurt a fly." Tiana let out a little chuckle. "I remember the one time you were screaming for your dad because there was a spider in the shower. And when he killed it, you screamed even more because you wanted to let it free outside."

Sophia's voice softened, but the tears were picking up speed again.

"I miss my dad."

"I think we all do, sweetie."

23

Ella
April 28, 2022

"Don't say a word unless I tell you it is okay. Don't answer any questions. Try your best to keep your expression neutral, no matter what they ask," Charlotte coached her as they waited in the bright interrogation room. Ella was kind of fascinated by the fact that they kept the lights so bright. Suspects probably caved a lot faster when fluorescent lights gave them a migraine.

"Is that why the people on trial always look that way? They were told not to react?"

"Ella, now is not the time," Charlotte moaned, exasperated.

Ella put her palms up and shrugged. "I was just asking."

"You need to be serious. I'm not sure what's gotten into you, but cut it out." Charlotte's words were sharp, but they didn't really reach Ella.

When she had gotten the call that the detective wanted to speak to her, she knew this situation could only go one of two ways. They clearly had found evidence, and they either believed she did it because of that evidence or they believed she was innocent. What she said didn't really matter, as long as she didn't say something incriminating. At least, that was what she convinced herself of on the silent car ride over.

"I got this." Ella sat up straighter and crossed her legs. She looked a little ridiculous in leggings from Old Navy and a flowy tank with a zip-up jacket. Charlotte had given her a look when she had gotten in the car, but she had chosen to ignore it. All her nice clothes were dirty at this point, and she couldn't do laundry until she could get back into the house.

Clemens opened the door, a file folder clutched in his sausage-link fingers. Ella wondered if there was a Mrs. Clemens, and how she would feel about him accusing a recent widow of murdering her husband.

"Thank you, ladies, for coming in today." His voice sounded warm, particularly because of his Southern accent. Ella found it repulsive.

"Cut the shit, Dave." Charlotte was sitting with her arms crossed. "What do you want?"

There was a small glimmer in Clemens's eye, and Ella shifted uncomfortably in the chair. He looked satisfied with himself. Charlotte glared over at Ella, her eyes telling her to stop moving.

"Charlotte, let a man enjoy his moment, will you?" Clemens smirked, and Ella felt herself squirming under his smugness. She wondered how common this banter was between the pair, and how much it probably pissed Charlotte off. Charlotte rolled her eyes and adjusted her gold bracelet. After what felt like an eternity to Ella, Clemens spoke: "We have new evidence."

Charlotte did a small clap. "Good job! I'm so proud." Her expression darkened on the flip of a dime as she removed her mask of enthusiasm. "I figured you would. That's kind of your job, you know."

Ella tried not to smile at Charlotte's rebuttal, but she was really glad at that moment that she had her as a lawyer.

"Oh, yes, I'm quite aware." He opened up the file folder and retrieved a plastic bag that appeared empty. He set it down on the table, and Ella stopped herself from leaning forward to get a better look. "We have found several pieces of this, mostly concentrated in the Mrs. Thomas's bedroom."

Charlotte reached out and grabbed the evidence bag, holding it up to the light. Ella tried not to look, but she couldn't help herself. The seemingly empty baggie held a single strand of bright-red hair.

24

Tiana
April 28, 2022

Since Sophia had left, Tiana had ordered herself some delivery from the local Mexican restaurant and had settled herself by the front door, waiting for it. A steak quesadilla and chips with queso was her go-to stress-eating meal. The session with Sophia hadn't necessarily gone badly, but the pressure had been building with each moment she had to keep Ella's children's sessions to herself. It was physically painful not to talk to her friend, especially when she knew she was going through so much, but Tiana also knew she would slip up if she called her to check in. She deeply regretted agreeing to meet with the kids, but at the same time, she was pleased they were getting the help they needed.

Tiana was scrolling through Facebook, catching up on all her friends' feeds, when a news article caught her eye.

LOCAL MISSING WOMAN CONNECTED
TO RECENT DEATH

Tiana blinked and clicked on the article, impatient as it loaded. Even though she didn't think anyone was really listening, she said a small prayer, hoping that the article wasn't connected to what she thought it was. Her eyes frantically scanned over the article summarizing Kelly Carter and how she hadn't been seen since Monday. Her parents described her as full of life, a metaphor that Tiana always found exceedingly ironic in these circumstances. Finally, she found the section she feared.

> *Sources close to the investigation claim they have discovered evidence connecting Carter to the recent death of Ryan Thomas. Detective David Clemens claimed that they do not have anything definitive at this time, but that they are looking for any tips regarding Kelly Carter or Ryan Thomas. Ryan Thomas was found dead Monday evening. Police have not yet announced a cause of death.*

Tiana was thankful that they hadn't mentioned the children, but everyone would know who they were regardless. All it took was a Facebook search to find Ryan's page, which was plastered with pictures of the family. His most recent picture was him with an arm around Sophia when she was inducted into the National Honor Society.

Now that she was in the black hole, she couldn't pull herself out. She searched for Kelly Carter on Google and found videos of police press conferences: one with the Carter family and another from tonight with the police chief posed at a podium.

Her thumb tapped the video and she turned the volume up. Most of the press conference was useless information that she had already read in the article. But as the conference wrapped up and the police chief was leaving the podium, a reporter shouted a question:

"What about the allegation that Kelly Carter's DNA was found in Ryan Thomas's bedroom?"

Tiana's heart stopped.

When the doorbell rang for her food delivery, Tiana had been staring at her phone's darkened screen for over five minutes.

25

Ella
April 28, 2022

"Mrs. Thomas, now is the time to come clean. The media is going to take this and run. It's better for your kids if you tell the truth now, get ahead of the story."

Ella blinked at Clemens, dumbfounded about what she was even supposed to say.

"I need a moment with my client." Charlotte set the bagged piece of Kelly Carter's hair down on the table.

"Of course." Dave pushed back his chair from the table and it scraped along the linoleum floor. He paused and turned back when he reached the door. "But the clock is ticking. Ticktock."

Charlotte rolled her eyes as the door shut behind Clemens. "He is such an asshole." She turned her entire body to face Ella. "Tell me everything."

"What?" Ella asked, her eyes staring down at the table where the evidence baggie had been.

"What do you know? What haven't you told me?" Charlotte looked irritated, her left foot tapping against the floor.

"About what?" Ella asked. Charlotte let out an exasperated sigh.

"He was having an affair? Have you heard her name before? How much of it did you know?"

"None of it. I didn't have a clue." Ella was having trouble keeping her breaths even, and it was all she could do to force herself to look Charlotte in the eye.

"You had *no* idea? There were no signs?"

Ella figured that Charlotte, as a recently divorced woman, couldn't imagine having no concerns about a marriage. Sam probably had a wandering eye, not that Ella had ever seen it herself, but it was probable.

"I mean he always kept in really good shape?" Ella forced herself to say, though that in and of itself didn't set off alarm bells. "He worked nights sometimes?" Her voice was high-pitched now, reaching a level of hysteria. This was all entirely ridiculous.

"Ella! Pull yourself together," Charlotte snapped.

"My husband was *not* a cheater." Ella slapped the table with her palms, pain shooting down her arms. The table budged slightly.

Ella's eyes narrowed, and she saw Charlotte stop short of speaking. Her face softened when the thought crossed her mind that maybe Charlotte was afraid of her. Maybe she was so afraid of her that she thought she could be a murderer.

"Sorry," Ella whispered.

Charlotte swallowed hard and shook her head. "It's an emotional time. I understand."

"I think I'd like to go back to my kids now." Ella tucked her blond hair behind her ears and smoothed her palms over the buttery fabric of her leggings.

"Would you like to make a statement to Clemens?"

Ella shook her head and tried to take deep breaths.

"Okay, hold on a minute." Charlotte pushed herself up from the chair, her heels clacking as she left the room. She was gone for a full minute before she came back. Those few moments were enough for panic to start rising up in her chest, making her feel like she was drowning. She could hear the sound of her heartbreak swelling in her ears, and she forced herself to regulate her breathing. Charlotte didn't seem to notice.

"I have good news. You can go back to your home."

Ella blinked. "I don't want to go back to that house . . ." She frantically wiped her tears away. "I don't want to be there without him."

26

Tiana
April 28, 2022

"An affair?" She shook her head in a slight motion that echoed her whisper. "Ryan would never. It doesn't make any sense."

Ella had texted Tiana when she left the police station, asking her to come to the hotel room. Tiana knew in her gut that the news was bad, but she didn't anticipate it being ridiculous enough to be an affair.

"I didn't think so either, but how do you explain that?" Ella copied Tiana's hushed tones. Nate and Sophia were just on the other side of the wall, and they had both decided it was best to keep this to themselves until they could wrap their heads around it. They would know about the affair sooner or later, but Ella wanted to finish processing it first.

Tiana paused at Ella's question. Her first thought when she had heard the press conference was far more sinister than an affair. There were a couple real answers that didn't include Ryan cheating on his wife.

"Stop that, what are you thinking?" Ella demanded, her eyes narrowing.

"I mean, I don't really know. It's all just speculation . . ." Tiana shrank away from her friend, sensing the fine line she was walking here.

"Tiana, you need to tell me." Ella swallowed, and when she spoke again, her voice was much softer. "If there is a chance that Ryan didn't break our vows"—Ella spun her wedding band on her finger—"I need to know."

"Okay." Tiana let out a deep breath. "There are a few possibilities I see, and none of them are good, but one is *way* worse."

"Give me the not-so-bad one."

"Kelly Carter could have been involved in his murder."

Ella nodded, looking hopeful as she considered the theory.

"It would make sense that her hair was in your home if it is the scene of the crime, and maybe she's not missing but is actually on the run because how does she explain her DNA at the scene?"

"That makes perfect sense. Why is that dumbass not suggesting that instead of trying to tear my husband's name apart?" Ella's forehead wrinkled as she spoke about Clemens, clearly disgusted by his very existence.

"Well, until they find her, they don't have anything to go on. She could very well be his mistress and be dead. It could be a coincidence. What makes the most sense with cases like this is that you found out about

Kelly, and maybe—" Tiana paused, trying to find a way to avoid saying it.

Ella finished it for her. "Killed them both. Right?"

Tiana gave a tight nod. "Or even a murder-suicide. Maybe Ryan couldn't take the guilt anymore. But if I was watching this go down on the news, and I didn't know any better, you would be my top suspect." Tiana feared maybe she did know better, but Ella wasn't at the top of her suspect list.

"But I have an alibi. I wasn't home all day long. I was at work. Surrounded by people."

"Yes, but that doesn't mean that maybe you didn't hire someone or maybe you had some man you were cheating on Ryan with do it."

"Okay, I get it," Ella scoffed, rolling her eyes away from Tiana.

"You asked." Tiana put her hands up, palms open. "I'm trying to help."

"What's the worst one?"

"What?" Tiana asked, placing her hands back down on her legs.

"What is the worst reason that Kelly's hair would be in my bedroom?" Ella enunciated each word.

"Ryan's secretly a serial killer or rapist, and she was his victim."

Ella blinked, and then laughed a full belly laugh that caused her to cover her own mouth to try to stop the kids from hearing. "Are you on drugs?"

Tiana frowned, and while she knew that Ella didn't seriously mean it, it still bothered her.

"Why would he be dead then?"

"Well, normally, I would guess suicide due to the guilt, but it sounds like the scene was way too violent for that. Maybe a vigilante caught him? I don't think it's a good theory. But it is always a possibility."

"And it's possible that I'll be the next president." Ella rolled her eyes and shook her head.

Silence fell over them as Tiana let Ella turn the ideas over in her head. She was just relieved that Ella hadn't asked about the kids' therapy sessions.

"You know I didn't kill him, right?" Ella asked, looking at Tiana out of the corner of her eye, not fully facing her.

"Why would you? Everyone loved him, most of all you."

Ella nodded, a few tears escaping again, even though they were still puffy from crying earlier. Tiana opened up her arms, and Ella leaned into her friend, holding herself rather than Tiana. Tiana held her close, tucking Ella's head under her chin.

"We'll figure out who did this to him. I know we will."

Ella didn't reply; she just kept crying. Tiana could feel the pit in the bottom of her stomach growing, and all she could wonder was how the hell she got herself so involved in this mess.

27

Ella
April 29, 2022

"They found hair from that missing woman in our house."

After spending the entire night tossing and turning, Ella had decided not to tell the kids that it was specifically in the bedroom she shared with Ryan. They could figure that out on their own if they wanted.

The conjoining hotel room was dead silent. Nate turned to look at Sophia, who was just staring straight ahead at Ella. Nate appeared concerned, but Sophia's hardened expression made Ella believe that she understood the implications. Of course, a girl would get it. In Ella's mind, every woman's biggest fear was their significant other cheating on them. Or at least, that had been Ella's until the police showed up and told her Ryan was dead.

"Do they have any leads?" Nate finally asked. Ella blinked, unsure of how to answer. "About the woman, I mean?"

Sophia crossed her arm and leaned back in the armchair. Ella's legs felt heavy, so she sat herself on the edge of the bed Nate was on.

"I don't know anything about that. I left before the detective could tell me any more."

Nate slowly nodded as if he didn't really understand.

"Good for you, Mom." Sophia gave a tiny smile, and Ella returned it, though it made her uncomfortable. "I'm proud of you for standing up for yourself. And for Dad."

The discomfort dissipated and Ella let herself smile wider now. She was actually setting a positive example for her daughter to not be intimidated by a man in power. That was a lesson she had never really planned on giving, but maybe there was the tiniest silver lining in all of this.

* * *

Ella felt dread weigh down her shoulders as she pulled into the driveway of their home. There was no police tape, and the outside of the home appeared undisturbed—just as it had when she had left for work on Monday morning. Four days had passed, and Ella was no closer to knowing what had happened to her husband, and it seemed like the police weren't either.

Before leaving the hotel that morning, Ella had called Charlotte to check for any updates, even though she knew there wouldn't be any.

"No, most of their force is wrapped up in the search for Kelly Carter. And since they think the two cases are connected, it doesn't seem like they are really too worried about looking into Ryan's case until they find out what happened to her."

Ella could hear the sound of Charlotte typing, and she wondered how many other people the woman could be representing right now. None of them could be half as serious as a murder.

"Okay." The irritation Ella felt leaked into her voice.

"I will call Clemens later today for an update. I'll text you with whatever he says."

"Thank you."

The line disconnected before Charlotte replied. Ella knew she was always busy; it was part of the reason Sam claimed they had gotten divorced. But real estate work didn't have exactly great hours either.

Now, the trio climbed out of the car. Nate had grabbed Ella's bag before she had a chance, and she gave him a sad smile in return.

With her hand on the front door, Ella shook. It took every ounce of strength in her to not turn around, jump back in the car, and drive away. But eventually, she forced it open.

The smell of bleach smacked her in the face and she couldn't breathe. She had forgotten about Tiana mentioning hiring a professional cleaner to remove all the biohazards, mostly because she couldn't be bothered to think about those details. Tiana had just stepped in, hired someone, let them in the house, paid them, and sent them on their way. After all of this, Ella owed her big time.

"I'm going to start a load of laundry. Can you guys gather anything dirty from the hotel?" Ella picked up her bag where Nate had left it on the kitchen floor.

"Sure thing," Sophia called, already on the search for her cat, Lily. Ella supposed that Tiana must have made sure she was taken care of as well. Nate nodded, picked up his own bag, and carried it down to the basement to dump his clothes into the washer.

Ella was left to her own devices in the kitchen. Her mouth felt dry, and when licking her lips didn't help, she opened the fridge to get a water. Ryan had been obsessed with plastic water bottles—he claimed the reusable ones always ended up stinking and tasting weird. Ella never had noticed, but she was thankful for his habit now. The convenience was helpful when her brain couldn't function well enough to manage the steps it took to find a reusable water bottle and fill it up.

A pungent odor from the fridge caught her attention immediately. There was some leftover taco salad in the back that Ella had prepared over a week ago. *Maybe two weeks*, she thought. Time was inconsequential now. She grabbed the first water bottle she saw and swung the door shut, deciding the fridge cleanout would be a task for another day and another version of herself.

The doorbell chirped and Ella nearly hit the ceiling. She coughed some water out of her lungs before glancing down at her outfit. Sweats and a t-shirt were not exactly her go-to for answering the front door, but it would have to do. She said a small prayer that it wasn't a reporter.

She glanced through the front curtain just to double-check it wasn't a news station trying to spring an inquisition on her about Kelly Carter and her *relationship* with Ryan. Instead, she found mild-mannered Sam standing in the doorway, flowers in his hand.

Ella opened the door, a small smile sneaking onto her face before the tears could hit. Sam and Ryan hadn't been best friends for life, but he had spent so much time in their lives the past few years, it seemed that way.

"Ella." His voice was soft. He held out his arms, and she fell into him, tears immediately staining the powder-blue fabric of his dress shirt. She rested her forehead against his shoulder, and his arms gripped her tightly, likely ruining half the flowers.

"I can't believe it."

Sam rubbed her back with his free hand in slow, small circles. "I know. Me neither."

There was a pause where neither of them could find any words. They pulled apart, and Ella stepped back from the doorway. Sam took a step into the foyer, a grim look on his face.

"I'm sorry I didn't come by sooner. I just—" His voice cracked as he fought back tears. "I didn't know what I could even say."

Ella nodded, her head bouncing quickly. "I know, I know." The last thing she wanted was for Sam to stay away from them because he felt guilty or anxious.

Mindlessly, she led him into the kitchen and took the flowers from him. He reached into the cabinet when it was too high up for her, grabbed a vase, and set it on the Formica countertop. She smiled and placed the white carnations into the tall, cylindrical vase, pulling out a few wilted pieces of baby's breath.

"You want a drink?" Ella asked, her arms resting against the edge of the counter.

"Do *you* want one?" Sam replied, raising one of his bushy eyebrows. She smiled in return and opened the fridge. She pulled out a light beer for him (his and Ryan's drink of choice) and a hard seltzer for herself. Her eyes glanced at the clock on the stove; it was just past noon. It was definitely too early to drink, especially under these circumstances, but her nerves needed it.

Sam moved into the living room from the kitchen and paused at the brown recliner that Ryan usually occupied. He seemed to think for a moment before continuing past it and sitting on the end of the sectional instead. Ella followed and settled on the opposite end, extending her legs over the chaise. Sam leaned forward, his elbows resting on his knees, the beer dangling from his fingertips.

"It's a bit weird, isn't it?" Sam asked.

Ella blinked and shook her head. "What do you mean?"

"Spending time together without him." He set the beer down on the coffee table, making sure to use a coaster.

Sam wasn't wrong. They had never really been together without Ryan, apart from maybe a car ride to meet up with him or waiting for him to come home from a house showing. A few minutes here and there, but always with the intention that Ryan would arrive soon. Ella gave a small nod.

"How are the kids handling it?" he asked, picking at a piece of skin on the palm of his hand.

"I'm not quite sure. I mean, they haven't opened up to me a ton. Tiana is talking with them, so that's at least a good thing." Ella let out a slow breath. "You know they found him, right?"

Sam's head snapped up from his hands. "What?"

"Well, I guess not. They got home from school after some study session and found him." After hearing Sophia's retelling to the cops, Ella could envision the scene—Sophia noticing that Ryan was home when his work shoes were lined up by the front door, maybe his rain jacket hanging on the banister. Maybe she called his name, or maybe she just wandered around in search of him. Finally, she decided he must be in the bedroom, and when she opened the door, she must have let out a scream so intense that Nate would know something was really wrong immediately.

"Ella—Ella!" Sam was calling her name when she snapped out of her trance.

"Sorry, I was just thinking about it."

"I can't imagine how hard that was for them. I wish it could have been me instead."

Ella nodded in agreement, but she didn't mean it. She was very glad she hadn't seen his body there. That was an image she definitely could never erase from the inside of her eyelids. Seeing the room afterward, covered in blood, was more than enough for her.

"Do they have any leads?"

Her stomach churned. For just a second, she had forgotten about Kelly Carter. About the fact that she had been inside Ella's home. Inside her bedroom.

"No," Ella forced out, which was the truth and a lie at the same time.

"I saw the news," Sam whispered, his mouth a straight line. Ella didn't bother answering. "Did they find that woman yet?"

"I don't think so."

The silence grew awkward once again, and Sam drained the rest of the beer. Ella thought he might stand up and excuse himself, but she didn't want him to leave. Sitting quietly with him was far better than tackling laundry and pretending her life was normal. But instead of standing, he sat back and made himself comfortable. Relief spread over Ella's face, erasing some of her wrinkles.

"Do you think he was cheating on me?" Ella asked, and Sam shrugged.

"If you would have asked me a week ago, I would've said, 'No way in hell.' Now, I don't know. It seems pretty damning, right?"

"I feel the same way." She let out a sigh. "I feel like everybody is so positive about everything. The cops were positive I killed him, and to a degree, they still are now that they found that hair. Most people are positive that he cheated on me. I'm not positive about anything though."

Sam nodded. "So, what do you think you know for certain then? There has to be something you can hold onto."

Ella thought for a moment. "I know *I* didn't kill him."

Sam let out an involuntary laugh. "Fair enough. What about the kids?"

"I know that—" The words caught in her throat. Sam's head tilted, intrigued. She swallowed hard. "The kids have been acting so different. I mean Sophia is acting so distant and angry, which is what I would expect. That's how I feel." Ella rested a hand on her chest.

"And Nate?" Sam asked, his voice quiet.

Ella lowered her voice too. "He's different. He's doing more to help. It's like he's on his best behavior."

"It's about time," he joked, but Ella didn't laugh.

"But—maybe I shouldn't say that." Ella shook her head and turned her gaze to the backyard.

"Say what?" Sam scooted forward to the edge of the couch, the cushion compacting under his weight.

"If I did something wrong, and I didn't want to get caught, I would be on my best behavior too."

28

Tiana
April 29, 2022

Tiana carried the takeout bags in her arms, trotting in the front door after unlocking it with her spare key.

"Delivery!" She called up the stairs, knowing the kids would be in their rooms. The plastic bag handles were digging into her arms, leaving angry red marks. She dropped them all on the counter, and Ella sat on the island with a seltzer in front of her.

"That kind of day, huh?"

"This is my third one. I'd offer you one, but there aren't any more."

Tiana raised her eyebrows but stayed silent as she began unloading containers of sushi.

"Okay, so I got all of your favorite rolls and some for the kids too." She paused as she moved onto the second bag of food. "And there is hibachi for leftovers since I know Nate will eat any sushi that isn't claimed within two hours."

"Thanks," Ella murmured, glancing down at her phone on the counter. Charlotte's name was displayed on the call, and Tiana frowned.

"Do you want me to give you some privacy?" She rested her hands on the counter in front of her, holding on for balance. She didn't know if she wanted to hear the kind of things she had at the police station on Tuesday. Despite loving true crime, it was a little different when it was someone you knew.

"Stay." Ella's voice broke as she spoke. She cleared her throat and swiped to answer the call. "Hello." She pushed the speaker button with her hand shaking.

"Hey. How are you doing?"

Even Tiana could tell that Charlotte wasn't really invested in the answer. She was asking out of politeness.

"I thought you said you would text an update—not call."

Tiana bit her bottom lip, the skin already feeling raw from the lapse in her normal skin-care routine. The past few days had thrown her off track.

"Yeah, well"—Charlotte cleared her throat—"this is a little bit bigger than what I was anticipating this morning."

Tiana's stomach lurched in anticipation.

"The autopsy was concluded today and the results were finalized." All the air was sucked out of the room in a second. Ella glanced up at Tiana, panic spreading in her eyes. She wasn't sure what either of them was afraid of, but the fear was there regardless. "There was one gunshot wound, which we had basically concluded based on the scene at the house, but it wasn't ruled as the primary cause of death."

"What?" Ella blinked at her phone, shaking her head. "I think I didn't hear you right. It *was* the cause of death."

Tiana's eyes narrowed in on Ella's face. The tiniest voice in the deep recesses of her brain wondered why Ella would be so insistent, but the larger, louder part of her brain said it was because she had seen the walls of the house. It was a large amount of blood. More than enough to kill someone.

"No. The shot was fired either postmortem or close to it, which means they were secondary to—"

"To what!" Ella snapped.

Tiana could imagine Charlotte rolling her eyes.

"The primary cause of his death was an overdose. The lab is still analyzing what specifically was used, but the coroner told me he thought it was likely caused by fentanyl."

Ella's eyebrows wove together and Tiana just about fell over. "Drugs!" she mouthed to Ella, who could do nothing but shake her head.

"That doesn't make any sense. It just doesn't." Ella stared down at the phone screen, watching the seconds tick by on the call. Ella crossed her arms firmly over her chest, shaking her head in a sweeping motion.

"I know. I thought the same thing."

"Is there anything else?" Ella asked, taking deep breaths to keep herself calm.

"As of now, that's it. But I have a bad feeling about something—" Charlotte began. She knew there was going to be something else. She could feel it in her bones.

"What? What is it?"

Tiana closed her eyes and rubbed the palms of her hands together, almost like she was praying. And for once in her life, she actually felt like she should say a prayer. Ella clearly needed it.

"Considering what we know about the scene and timeline—he overdosed on some kind of drug and then he was shot—there wouldn't be nearly as much blood because of this order."

Ella rolled her eyes. Even though Charlotte was trying her best to spell it out for her, she wanted to get to the point.

"The blood spatter analysis will likely show that he wasn't the only one at the scene who was shot." Charlotte paused and took an audible breath. "And with how much blood there was, I think he wasn't the only one killed."

29

Ella
April 29, 2022

"I'm sorry, I really just want to be alone right now." Ella stood in the doorway, and Tiana, on the front porch.

"Are you sure? We can talk through this." It almost felt like Tiana wanted to stay to make herself feel better, not Ella. A little bit of anger bubbled under the surface, which Ella decided was mostly because of the situation and had nothing to do with Tiana.

"No. I just need to process alone." Ella tried to muster her best reassuring smile, and seemingly convinced, Tiana nodded.

"Okay. Text me tomorrow, okay? Now that the autopsy is done, you will have to make some arrangements."

Ella nodded, but she knew what Tiana really meant was *she* would take charge of the arrangements, since thus far, Ella hadn't been able to function at a high enough level for something like that. At this point, she was just trying to survive each day. Ella tried to not feel shame about this fact. Even as a widow, she was still a mother. If her kids needed her, she didn't really feel like she could be there. And there wasn't exactly an instruction manual on how to tell your kids that their father overdosed.

Tiana turned and walked down to her car, and Ella shut the door without looking back. Her eyes stung, but there were no tears. She felt shock more than anything. Two people had died in her bedroom. And she didn't even know who one of them was. Nate had come down the stairs, followed closely by Sophia.

"Food is here?" Nate asked, barely glancing at Ella at first. She didn't respond; she just stood in the foyer, looking straight ahead toward the kitchen. "Mom?" He touched her arm.

Sophia paused, too, halfway to the kitchen already.

"I'm fine . . ." The words fell out of her mouth, both syllables raspy.

"What's going on?" Sophia's eyes darted out the front door.

"I don't even know what to say at this point." Ella shook her head, and Nate placed his hands on both her shoulders.

"Look at me, Mom. Whatever it is, you can tell me." His voice was a little frantic, and his fingers dug into her when she didn't answer.

"Your dad overdosed."

Nate and Sophia glanced at each other before looking back to their mother, the concern on their faces multiplying.

"Drugs? But the bedroom was—" Sophia started. Nate held up a hand to stop her. She didn't need to tell *them* what the bedroom looked like.

"That's what the autopsy showed." Ella shrugged, but she couldn't even feel her body moving. It felt like she was underwater.

"Then it's wrong. Obviously." Nate had dropped his hands from Ella's body, and now his arms were crossed in front of him. Rather than appearing defensive, it made him look like he was hiding. Sophia nodded in agreement behind him.

"I thought so, too, but maybe we didn't know him as well as we thought." Ella imagined Ryan's presence in the house. It was hard to picture him being here now, hearing her say these things. Logically, she knew it had to be true, but emotionally, she refused to believe it. Her husband had never even touched anything harder than Tylenol or whiskey. At this point, he must have had an entire life that he hid from her.

"I don't believe it." Sophia shrugged, dismissing the idea entirely. Both kids held steady, not budging on their beliefs about their father. Ella wondered what it said about her that she was willing to accept it as fact.

"Come on, let's eat something, and then we can figure out where to go from here. You look like you need it." Nate put a hand on his mother's shoulder, hoping to guide her into the kitchen. She moved slowly, giving into his touch.

Ella hadn't had anything to eat that day, unless the hard seltzers counted, which if anything, they made her feel worse. Sushi sounded completely unappetizing, so Nate served her some of the fried rice and chicken. Once Ella was situated at the island, Sophia grabbed her a glass of water, and Ella could feel Sophia's eyes staring at her from across the counter. She couldn't maintain eye contact for more than a second or two. They all ate in silence, none of them on their phones, just sitting in the realization that their father might have not been who they thought.

Over the next 15 minutes, Ella picked at her food, taking a few bites but mostly moving it around the plate. Whenever she looked up, the kids were doing the same. Finally, Sophia spoke.

"I personally don't think we should put any energy into this. We can't do anything right now, and I don't think we should spend time thinking about it."

Ella didn't look up from her plate.

"I agree. We can wait to get more information. I mean, if someone shot Dad, maybe they gave him drugs against his will? Or made him take them," Nate suggested.

Ella found herself nodding. Sophia nodded emphatically.

"Maybe." Her words carried a small bit of hope.

"So, we need to wait for more information," Sophia concluded, pushing her plate slightly away.

"I am okay with that." Ella's voice was a step above a whisper.

"Do you need help with anything, Mom?" Nate asked, his face gentle.

Ella sat, thinking for a brief moment. One side of her mouth turned upward, but it was nowhere near a full smile.

"I never did laundry." Ella let out a soft chuckle, but it just sounded like she was choking back tears.

"I can do that," he offered, already beginning to stand.

Ella frowned; the thought of her son touching her dirty clothes was making her more nauseous than she already was. Sophia touched Nate's shoulder and jumped up from the stool.

"I'll take care of that. Maybe you can put away the food?" Sophia was already heading for the basement steps. Nate nodded, and Ella cleared her throat. Sophia launched herself into action and her footsteps echoed off the wood of the steps.

"If you wouldn't mind, I think there's some stuff that needs to be thrown away in there."

Nate nodded, and a look of determination spread on his face as he began putting lids on the takeout. "I got this. Why don't you go lie down?"

Ella hauled herself off the island stool and moved to the stairs without another word. She couldn't help feeling like she was useless as a parent. Had Ryan made parenting so much easier? Her kids were springing into action, holding their family together. Between them and Tiana, she didn't have to worry about anything. The thought was both comforting and destructive. What use was she if everyone else could get by without her?

About halfway up the stairs, she stopped.

I can't stay in there, she thought. Flashes of the bloody comforter appeared inside her head. The comforter was probably thrown out. The blood would be gone. But the ghost of what had happened four days ago lingered. Ella sighed and moved up the rest of the stairs before going into the spare bedroom, hoping she could finally get some sleep.

30

Tiana
May 2, 2022

"I'm sorry, Sophia, but I need to talk about this with you. It's not professional, but I can't help it." Tiana sat in her armchair, staring at Sophia, who clutched a pillow in her lap.

"The drugs, right?" Sophia asked, shaking her head. Her face was mystified as if she was gossiping about a celebrity.

"Yes. There is *no* way your dad did drugs."

"I mean, anything is possible. People hide secrets forever that nobody they love knows about."

Tiana bit her bottom lip. She knew this was true, but she thought of herself as an open book. Her mind focused on herself for a moment, and she thought about the session notes she had written for Nate. How she had kept them intentionally vague. How she had omitted so much.

"I guess you're right."

"I know." Sophia shrugged. When in public, she was typically mild mannered, but with her family, she was self-assured. Almost cocky.

"How are you feeling about the memorial tomorrow?"

When Tiana and Ella had discussed the arrangements, she hadn't brought up the phone call from Charlotte. It didn't feel right, and Ella didn't say a word about it. Tiana had fought off the urge to ask Charlotte all weekend. Instead, she dove headfirst into obituaries and scoured for photographs showcasing Ryan's life. They had kept every photo digitally for the past ten years, so it was relatively easy to do, but mentally difficult.

There was one photo in particular that crushed her. It was Sophia's eighth birthday party, from before Tiana had even known them. The birthday cake was lit on the table, and Sophia was perched on Ryan's lap. Her eyes were wide and her hands were up in the air. You can tell she was in the middle of giggling. Ryan was smiling too.

Tiana had taken a break after seeing that one.

"I'm not looking forward to it. I'd rather not go."

This caught Tiana's attention. "What?"

"I don't want to go and listen to all these people apologize for him dying. Half of them will just be there because they feel like they have to, and the other half is there because they want to gossip about it. It doesn't mean anything."

Sophia did have a point. Tiana herself hated anything even remotely close to a funeral, and it was made even worse when she knew that it was one that would make her cry. She spent every day leading up to one dreading it just because she would be crying before everyone. She wasn't certain why she was afraid of being vulnerable, but at least she knew it was an issue.

"I think you're right. Did you talk to your mom about this?" Tiana settled back in her chair, her fingers running over the simple gold bracelet she had on her left wrist.

"Of course not. It's not like I can just choose not to go. It would look awful, and we don't need any extra attention on us."

Tiana opened her mouth to speak, but changed her mind, her lips forming into a frown. They stayed like that for a moment before Tiana decided what she wanted to say.

"That's so unfair to you. That you have to sit here and try to figure out what you can and cannot do simply because it might look bad. Nobody should have to live like that."

"Well, when they're trying to pin a murder on your mother, you kind of have to."

Tiana felt the awkwardness of the conversation begin to slip in again. How was she meant to reply to this when she was best friends with her mother?

"Your mother did not do this. And with time, the police will know that too." A small smile grew on Tiana's face, feeling satisfied that she had settled on a good response.

Sophia leaned forward in the chair, the pillow tumbling from her lap to the floor. "It's nice to think that. But at the end of the day, who really knows?"

31

Ella
May 3, 2022

Sam was standing in the foyer when Ella finally gathered up the courage to make her way downstairs for the funeral. Last night, she had sent Sam a text because her nerves had felt like they were on fire. Her mind kept flashing back to their meeting in the living room last week, and the awkwardness that accompanied it. But apart from the kids, being around Sam was the closest she could get to Ryan, and she knew she would need it for today.

"Thanks for agreeing to drive." She reached the bottom of the stairs and flattened her black dress with a hand, smoothing out any last-minute wrinkles. It had short sleeves, and she had chosen a cheap gold necklace, the first piece of jewelry Ryan had ever bought for her, to wear. Her hair was straightened, hiding the gold studs she had to match. In her other hand, she clutched a pair of black sunglasses.

"Of course. I would have offered if I had thought of it first." Sam gave a tiny smile.

That was the thing about Ryan: He always was thinking ahead. He paid attention to details and tried to have everything sorted out so Ella wouldn't have to worry about a thing. She didn't think there were many men on this planet like that.

"Are the kids in the living room?" Ella asked.

"I don't know. I just got here." Sam stuck his hands in the pockets of his black dress pants.

Ella moved toward the kitchen. "Guys, are you ready?" Ella turned the corner into the living room with Sam trotting a few feet behind.

Ella found Nate and Sophia in the living room, Nate's large form nearly swallowing Sophia whole in a hug. The pair was nearly silent as Nate rubbed his hand up and down his sister's shoulders while her body shook with sobs. Ella stood in the doorway for a moment, unsure of what to do. The kids hadn't shown much emotion this entire time, and she didn't want to scare them off.

Slowly, she made her way across the carpeted floor and reached out to the children. Nate took one arm off Sophia so he could pull his mother into the hug. Sophia didn't move her head from Nate's chest so Ella didn't quite fit properly, but she did her best. Tears were pricking her own eyes, but she tried her best not to give in to them. There would be enough crying today without her losing it in front of her kids.

After a few minutes, Sam cleared his throat in the doorway. Ella pulled away from the kids and turned to him.

"Sorry," he said sheepishly. "But I think we need to get going."

Ella glanced at the black watch on her wrist and nodded. She turned around and hugged the kids once more, tightly, then pulled back. "We need to go."

Nate finally dropped his arms from Sophia, and when she pulled back, her bright-red face was coated with tears. Ella moved to the kitchen counter, grabbed her purse, and pulled out a small packet of tissues.

"Take these."

Sophia grabbed the pack, fumbling to get a tissue out before Nate stepped in and helped her. Ella's heart felt like it was crumbling all over again. Seeing her kids feeling so broken made her feel so many things, but mostly like a failure. It was her job to protect her kids from this, and she couldn't. There had been no way to prevent this.

"Let's go." Ella stepped past Sam and headed out the front door toward his car that was parked in the driveway. It startled her for a moment, seeing the exact same model car as Ryan's, down to the same color. Ella had been avoiding the garage since they got home, so she hadn't seen Ryan's car, but she assumed it was still in there, untouched. Over a year ago, Ryan had gone on this kick about how research showed that statistically, realtors who drove a Lexus closed on more homes, and Ella tried to suggest that perhaps the drivers just worked harder and could afford a Lexus because they made more sales. But once Ryan told Sam about the 'research,' he jumped on board and leased one himself.

Sam walked around and opened the passenger door for Ella, and she settled down onto the leather seat, slid on the black sunglasses, and said a little prayer that everything would go smoothly. She told herself it would be over before she knew it, but a tiny part of her told her the funeral was just the beginning of something new. Something much worse.

32

Tiana
May 3, 2022

"Thank you for coming." Tiana was stationed at the entrance to the funeral parlor. They had decided to have Ryan cremated, but not until after the memorial service. His dark oak casket was shut, light bouncing off the polish. The decision to keep the casket closed had been Ella's. They had gone back and forth on it a few times before finally, Ella spat out what she was really thinking:

"The kids already saw him dead once. I'm not making them go through that again!"

Tiana had to admit she had a point. Seeing Ryan like that again could retraumatize them. So now, they were all gathering to say goodbye to a wooden box instead of a real person. While Tiana ultimately agreed with Ella, it made the entire memorial seem even more pointless. When she died, she wanted nothing. Screw closure. People could go to therapy for that.

"Thanks for coming." She awkwardly smiled at who she thought might be one of Ryan's aunts.

As Ella walked through the door with Sam, Tiana felt the stress disappear from her shoulders.

It's about time, she thought. She wanted to be compassionate, but she was pretty pissed she was stuck welcoming guests without Ella.

Ella didn't remove the sunglasses as she approached Tiana. "Sorry we're late. We had a"—she cleared her throat—"moment at home before we left." Her voice sounded hollow, and Tiana felt chills bite at the skin of her back.

"It's okay." Tiana felt a bit bad for her internal reaction. It wasn't like she could truly understand what they all were going through. Sam's face appeared over Ella's shoulder.

"You should probably step inside. People are going to want to talk to you."

Ella stepped back from Tiana, almost crashing into Sam in the process. Nate and Sophia had already disappeared inside the parlor, probably blending into the crowd to avoid having to talk to people.

"Do you want me to come in there with you?" Tiana asked, her foot ready to step after her.

Ella reached up, pulled off the sunglasses, and fiddled with them. Her eyes didn't meet Tiana's, but she could see that they were a little puffy. "I think I'll have Sam up there with me. He knew most of Ryan's friends and coworkers."

Tiana felt a pang in her chest. Throughout all the planning, she figured that she would be at Ella's side during the receiving line, supplying tissues and hugs when necessary. Now, she was demoted to greeter—a job she would assign to a family member she disliked.

Tiana gave a tight nod instead of vocalizing all the feelings she had. Sam reached out, put a hand on Tiana's shoulder, and gave it a gentle squeeze, offering a simultaneous smile.

After a few minutes, she stepped to the side to take a look. She spotted Ella and Sam next to the casket, his hand resting on her upper back while she spoke to somebody Tiana didn't recognize.

She let out a slow and deep breath. Even after trying everything, it felt like she was getting demoted as a friend too.

33

Ella
May 3, 2022

"We are just absolutely devastated by this." Ryan's boss, Greg Hartman, was shaking his head, reminding Ella of one of those birds that dip its head up and down to drink water. His face was naturally ruddy, and his eyes appeared slightly watery. Ella figured it wasn't from crying, just from being older. His wrinkled hands clasped hers, and Ella longed to pull them away from his cold skin.

"Thank you," Ella managed.

"Mr. Hartman, I will be in later today to take a look at his clients," Sam offered. Hartman waved his hand. Ryan had always lived in clutter and disorganization when Ella wasn't around, so she could only imagine the mess that his office would be.

"I've already had Sarah organize them. But—" He paused, looking uncertain. He glanced behind him and then continued, "we do need you to finish the Geller's paperwork."

Ella looked at Sam, who nodded with an enthusiasm that made Ella uncomfortable.

"Absolutely, sir. It'd be my honor." Sam gave a bashful smile.

"Such a shame that Ryan couldn't be the one to close." Hartman turned away and shook his head again.

Ella turned to Sam with her eyebrows raised. "Geller?"

The smile disappeared from Sam's face. "Ryan didn't mention it, huh? It was our first business real-estate deal. He was pretty excited about it."

"No, he didn't say a damn thing about it." Ella's eyes narrowed, trying to read his facial expressions.

"Oh." Sam blew out a deep breath and shoved his hands in his pockets. He frowned. "I guess the cat is out of the bag. He was trying to keep it a surprise. I think he was going to use some of it to start a college fund for the kids—or at least for Sophia."

His joke fell flat.

"He was keeping a secret?" Images flicked through Ella's head. If this was a secret, what other things were there? How many bad secrets did he keep for every good one?

"Yeah. He said something about a big anniversary trip too."

Ella swallowed down her bitterness. At the end of the day, she thought Ryan meant well. He was kind and loving. But still, the idea that Ryan had a secret life lingered. A life with Kelly Carter. A life with drugs. A life without her. Most of all, she felt anger. Regardless of why Ryan died, Ella was starting to believe that somehow it was his fault.

34

Tiana
May 3, 2022

"Can we ride home with you?" Ella whispered in Tiana's ear as the memorial was dying down. There had been no service—Ella didn't think she was able to deliver a eulogy, and she was pretty sure she didn't want anyone else to either. At the end of the day, it was just a viewing without any actual views.

"Yeah, absolutely." Tiana tilted her head to the side, curious, but she kept her thoughts on the back burner for now. Sam approached and opened his arms for another hug from Ella.

Tiana watched, noticing how Ella's arms loosely surrounded his body and pulled back almost as quickly as she could. Ella's face scrunched up when Sam's suit jacket brushed against her face.

"Ready to go?" Sam asked, jingling his car keys in his pocket.

Ella met Sam's eyes directly. "We're actually going to ride home with Tiana."

Tiana blinked, caught off guard by Ella's new tune. She had walked into here like Sam and she were best buds. Like he was her replacement. Or even worse, a smaller part of her brain had told her maybe he was Ryan's replacement. Maybe Ella knew more about his death than she was letting on. But now, she could sense the chill in Ella's words.

"Oh. Alright. That's fine. I need to stop into the office anyway." He recovered well from the surprise, and Tiana wondered if he was disappointed at all. "Give me a call if you want to chat."

Ella nodded but didn't reply. Sam slowly turned on his one foot before shrugging it off and exiting toward the parking lot.

"What's going on? Did something happen?" Tiana was dying to know what Sam had done to get on Ella's bad side because maybe that would help her figure out what to avoid. It struck her how much she felt like she had become Ella's spouse in that moment. With Ryan gone, she had stepped right in to support her without being asked. It was possible that Ella didn't want her as involved as she was. If she pushed too hard, she would lose Ella—and just as importantly, the kids.

"I have a bad feeling." Ella's voice was barely above a whisper. Tiana raised her eyebrows and leaned in closer, her curls touching Ella's bob.

"About what?"

"About *Sam*." Ella's eyes met hers, filled to the brim with fear.

Tiana leaned back, surprised. "Like he was involved?" Her voice was a whisper now too.

Ella ran her tongue over her lips and then gave the slightest nod.

"Why?" Confusion erupted on Tiana's face as she shook her head slightly. Accusing Sam of murdering Ryan was about as ridiculous as Ryan doing drugs.

"Let's talk at home." Ella stepped toward the exit and wove through the crowd, avoiding people trying to catch her heading out the door.

Tiana frowned and hurried after Ella, her heels clicking against the floor. She reached out and tapped Sophia on the shoulder.

"Time to go," Sophia said. When Tiana glanced back, Sophia pulled her brother behind her.

The three of them trailed after Ella, making their way out the front doors. Ella had already reached Tiana's car by the time her eyes adjusted to the brightness.

As Tiana made her way around to her side of the car, she heard Ella pull on the passenger door handle before Tiana had a chance to unlock it. Her eyes met Ella's, where she caught a glimpse of pain and a few tears before Ella forced her sunglasses back on.

The car ride was absolutely silent, the kids sitting in the back on their phones, Ella staring at her lap, and Tiana constantly adjusting the air conditioning and vents. When she wasn't touching the air, she was biting her fingernails, a habit she had kicked two decades ago. Finally, the house came into view.

Once the car was in park, Sophia pushed open her door, probably eager to get out of the oppressive silence of the car. Nate leaned forward, his head between the two front seats. Tiana didn't turn around but instead eyed him in the rearview mirror. Ella turned slightly but made no eye contact. Instead, her eyes seemed to space out while staring at the leather center console.

"At least it's over, right? One less thing to go through?" he asked. Tiana found his attempt to comfort his mother sweet, but at the same time, so naïve. Tiana didn't have to see through Ella's sunglasses to know she was rolling her eyes. Tiana turned and touched Nate's shoulder for just a second.

"Yes. It's not over, but you guys have gotten through one more thing."

Nate gave a small nod before climbing out of the car. Once he disappeared inside the house, Ella took off her sunglasses and stared at them in her hands.

"So what happened?" Tiana's voice cracked halfway through her question.

"Apparently—" Ella let out a loud huff "—Ryan had a big commission coming his way. Soon. By the sounds of it, maybe the biggest ever."

Tiana blinked. "That would have been awesome."

"Yeah." Ella didn't explain her thought. Tiana sat, her hands resting in her lap, thinking.

"So why are you mad at Sam?"

"Tiana, think for a second." Ella shook her head, looking frustrated. Tiana stared out at the garage door, turning the idea over in her head.

"No," she spat, her face scrunching together. "You don't think Sam did it?"

Ella nodded her head dramatically.

"To get the commission instead?" Tiana finished, glancing down at her bitten-down fingernails. "Shit."

The pieces made sense. Charlotte had annihilated Sam in the divorce. The only thing she had left him was the cottage they stayed at sometimes in the summer. Tiana had been there once, a few years back. It was a decent size and not too far from town, but it wasn't exactly the ideal living situation. The plumbing was finicky, the bugs were awful, and there was no cell phone service. Sam had ended up renting an apartment in town, and the cottage was relatively untouched. He could use some money, and depending on how large the commission was, it could make sense.

"But he wouldn't do that, right?" Tiana finally asked even after realizing he was the best suspect they had.

"People have done worse for less."

35

Ella
May 3, 2022

"I just got off the phone with Clemens." Charlotte's voice echoed as Ella switched her to speakerphone. Tiana had just left, the kids were hiding up in the rooms, and she was flayed out on the sectional, more tired than she had ever been in her life.

"And?" Ella asked, her eyes shut as she let out a yawn.

"There's more news."

Ella's eyes snapped awake. She forced herself to sit up, clasping the phone tightly.

"I guess Clemens finally got around to questioning Ryan's boss. There was a large—"

"Commission, I know. I just heard about it at the funeral." Ella frowned; she figured the news wasn't as big as she hoped.

"Good." Charlotte paused. "I mean, good that you know. I don't know if this will lead them anywhere, but it means they are finally paying some attention to Ryan's case and doing their jobs."

"Charlotte, do you know who they gave the big client to?" Ella said her words slowly and carefully. The phone was silent long enough that Ella checked to make sure they hadn't been disconnected.

"Sam?" she finally asked, pain in her voice.

"Sam," Ella confirmed, and for the first time today, she felt sick to her stomach. "Is this going to be a conflict of interest?"

"No—I mean, I don't think so. I'm not connected to him anymore, legally speaking. I have your interest more in mind than his, so I think it will be a nonissue."

It was the first time that Ella had heard Charlotte's voice lacking confidence.

"So do you think Sam is a person of interest?" Ella asked, running her hand through her hair, her fingers getting caught on a knot near the back that needed to be brushed out.

"Technically, he seems like the only candidate, apart from the suggestion that you are a scorned lover. So yes, he is probably on their radar. But at the end of the day, it's a coincidence. Without solid evidence, they have nothing."

Charlotte's words relaxed the tension in Ella's shoulders. It didn't make sense that Sam would tear up a friendship that had lasted years just for a quick buck. If he had asked, maybe Ryan would have even split the commission with him.

"That's good." Ella ran her hand along the cotton fabric of her black dress. So far, she hadn't found the energy to change.

Charlotte attempted to be gentle with her next words, but they still had a tinge of brashness. "That still doesn't explain Kelly Carter's hair."

36

Tiana
May 4, 2022

"How many more of these sessions do you think we will have to do?" Nate asked, staring down at his hands. He cracked each knuckle, moving from finger to finger. Tiana hated the sound cracking knuckles made, but she tried not to show it on her face.

"I would say that's up to you, but I bet your mom might have something to say about it." Ella hadn't discussed it with Tiana, but surely it couldn't go on forever. She couldn't expect free therapy indefinitely. However, it was only one day after the funeral, so the kids probably had a long way to go.

Nate nodded along, staring at the floor in front of him. Tiana leaned forward just a bit.

"I think this is important, though." Tiana played with a black felt-tip pen, uncapping and recapping it with her thumb. She kept her eyes on Nate. "What do you want to get out of therapy?"

Nate's eyes scanned the room. "I guess I have trauma or whatever." He held up air quotes as he spoke.

Tiana cracked a small smile. "I would say probably yes, you do."

"I saw a lot of things that day I didn't want to see."

Tiana nodded, sympathy for Nate etched into her forehead. "I'm going to be very honest with you, Nate."

His brown eyes looked up, glittering.

"Trauma is a very difficult thing to deal with and to treat. Everybody is different. For some people, they need a long time to even be able to talk about it. Others are ready to talk right away. I don't know where you stand, so what we do with that trauma is all up to you. We can talk about other things if you like. Or we can skip over the details."

Nate nodded, biting his bottom lip. The skin was so chapped that Tiana could see it from where she was sitting.

"Whatever you want." She offered an encouraging smile.

"I want to talk about it. That day."

Even after all she had told him, Tiana felt like all the air was sucked out of her lungs. She wasn't sure if *she* was ready to hear about it yet.

"Okay, I'll just sit and listen." Tiana didn't know what else she could handle doing, but she had to listen to what he really saw that day, to the parts that haunted him each waking moment, and some of the sleeping ones too. He hadn't mentioned having nightmares, but Tiana couldn't imagine not having them.

"I had a funny feeling the minute we walked in the door." Nate stared out the front window to the street.

The curtains offered a small amount of privacy, but not complete opacity. He watched without talking as a woman walking her dog passed by. Tiana wished she had left Ollie out of his crate this morning. They could both probably use the emotional support right now.

"The house didn't smell right. It wasn't bad, exactly. Just off. Everybody's house has a smell. Even yours. It smells like you. Or maybe it's the other way around." Nate shrugged, shaking his head slightly. "Anyway, it didn't smell like any of us, or the way it normally does. It smelled like someone else had been there."

Tiana leaned forward, intrigued now. The gory details were the bit she wasn't looking forward to, but this, this was useful information.

"I headed up the stairs right away without really thinking about it."

Tiana felt her breath catch in her throat. The details weren't crystal clear, but she was pretty sure that Sophia had claimed she was the first upstairs when they had spoken to the detectives. Her face must have given away her thoughts because Nate stopped.

Tiana frowned. "Sorry. I just got distracted."

She hoped she covered up her lapse.

Nate shook his head. "I have a question."

Tiana cursed herself for interrupting his thoughts. She needed to know what happened next, and why it didn't line up with the story they had told the police. "Go ahead." She managed to keep her voice casual despite the adrenaline entering her bloodstream.

"We have client-patient confidentiality, right? Or whatever it's called."

Tiana's lips pressed together firmly. "Yes."

"And that means you can't tell anybody what goes on here?" Nate clarified, staring directly into Tiana's eyes. She blinked.

"Yes." There were stipulations, but Tiana didn't mention them. If he was a threat to himself or others, then she was required to break that confidentiality. The police could also potentially subpoena her session notes, but she had decided after the first session to keep those vague. She had already decided to protect Nate no matter what. And whatever had happened, she had a feeling deep down that his involvement was minimal. He was a sweetheart at his core—a side he didn't show many people. A side she felt privileged to see. If she was honest, she was afraid if she didn't protect that core, this situation would destroy him entirely.

Nate's body visibly relaxed, and for just a moment, Tiana felt at ease too. Until he spoke again.

"Then let me tell you what really happened."

37

Ella
May 4, 2022

Charlotte had called Ella just a few minutes after Nate
had left for his session with Tiana.

"They want us down there immediately. Clemens
wouldn't tell me what it was about, but they clearly
found something new. My guess is they want to ask us
about Sam's connection to everything. But it could also
be something completely out of left field. I hate this
shit!" Ella could hear Charlotte smack her steering
wheel. "They want to keep us in suspense. They think
they can just dangle a carrot out, and we'll—"

Ella had tuned Charlotte out by that point, her brain
running down a laundry list of what Clemens could
know. Dread weighed her stomach down.

Now, Dave Clemens finally slid inside the
interrogation room. She could tell by the smug little
smile on Clemens's face that her instincts had been

right. They had found something bad. She had never wanted to punch somebody so badly.

"Are you going to tell us why you dragged us here?" Charlotte barked.

"I don't mind if I do."

Clemens reached into his file folder that he always carried around like it was a fashion statement and pulled out some photographs. When they were set down on the table, it was clear they were photographs of the crime scene, particularly of the blood splatter. Ella could feel Charlotte tense next to her. She had mentioned that she thought there was too much blood, especially for how Ryan had died.

"Before I start, do you have anything you'd like to say, Mrs. Thomas?" He tilted his head to the side, his face an obvious imitation of politeness and concern. The fire in his eyes waited to burn her to a crisp.

Ella simply shook her head, uninterested in giving Clemens anything to feed off of. He was just like a vampire, but she was pretty sure he had the seduction skills of a cardboard box.

"Analysis has come back on the blood found at the scene. There was a lot of it to sort through." Clemens glanced up from the photographs to gauge Ella's reaction. She didn't flinch. "And of course, we found your husband's blood. That was a given." He shrugged. With each word, Ella could feel her blood pressure rising, the whooshing in her ears like the sound of an ultrasound machine heartbeat. He was toying with her.

"And?" Charlotte asked, trying to play it off as nothing, though Ella knew that she was probably eager to know what they had discovered.

"We found somebody else's blood too." Clemens didn't look down at the photograph, but his eyes were locked on Ella, barely blinking. She tried her best not to give him the satisfaction.

"Dave," Charlotte warned, "don't waste our time here. If you want our cooperation, you need to earn it."

A sly smile spread on Clemens's lips.

Crossing his arms, he leaned back in his chair. "I don't know how much I will need your cooperation after this. I have a pretty good idea of what happened now."

Ella's heart dropped down into her stomach. For a brief moment, she let herself hope that the smug asshole had actually done his job, and that he wasn't playing cat and mouse with her.

"Do you, now? Then maybe we should go."

Charlotte started to stand, but Ella remained glued to the chair. Her strength and confidence were gone now, outweighed by her need to know the truth.

"Doesn't look like your client wants to leave, does it?"

Charlotte let out an exasperated sigh and settled back down in the chair. She stopped responding now, and Dave leaned forward again, interlocking his fingers.

"It was Kelly Carter's blood. All. Over. Your. Bedroom."

The temperature in the room rose, and Ella thought she might pass out. It wasn't a fluke then. It wasn't a single hair that had somehow been tracked into her home. Kelly Carter was there, with her husband, and now they were both dead. Or probably dead. Her eyes glanced down at the photographs. It was an awful lot of blood.

"Care to explain that?"

Ella slumped back in her chair. So, he hadn't really made some amazing discovery. Just more evidence, but no suspect. Other than her.

"I believe you are forgetting that my client has an alibi." Charlotte reached out under the table and squeezed Ella's arm, telling her so many things at once. *Don't say a word. Don't worry about this.*

The smile that spread over Clemens's face again dismissed Charlotte's comfort. There was more. There had to be.

"Oh, I don't believe that Mrs. Thomas got her hands dirty at all. She doesn't seem the type." Clemens glanced at Charlotte, then gave all his attention to Ella. She could feel him boring holes into her.

"I don't like what you are suggesting. And if you don't have any evidence to prove this outrageous accusation, we're leaving. Maybe you could actually do your job, then, instead of pursuing outlandish theories."

Ella was the first to stand now, forcing herself up to her feet. Charlotte followed, and Clemens didn't say a word as they slipped out the door.

* * *

"Mom!" Sophia yelled from the living room.

Every time one of the kids yelled now, her heart almost came up through her throat as she envisioned every completely awful thing that could be happening. In record time, she hefted herself out of the spare bedroom and down the stairs, her socks sliding when she rounded the foyer.

Sophia was standing in the living room, sporting her Scooby-Doo pajama set (which she had mostly outgrown but refused to stop wearing) with her phone in her hand. Her eyes were glued to some news broadcast on the television.

Nate, likely unable to ignore his sister's yell, appeared behind Ella in the living room and leaned against the archway.

It was a full minute before Ella's eyes settled on the screen. A reporter stood outside a wooded area, a driveway vaguely visible behind her. Twilight had settled around the reporter, but it was clear they had pulled out the floodlights to record, causing the background to be mostly obscured. Her eyes scanned the rotating banner on the bottom of the screen:

BREAKING NEWS . . . BODY FOUND . . .

"Police have not made an official comment yet on the identity of the body, but it was discovered during a search party organized to find Kelly Carter, a 29-year-old woman who has been missing since early last week." The reporter echoed in Ella's head, making her feel dizzy and overheated at the same time. "The coroner has been called to the scene, and it appears the body was transported to the coroner's office. It is likely the police will be making a statement sometime tomorrow about this discovery."

Ella stood still, trying to compensate for her heart beating out of her chest. A small part of her had hoped that Kelly would be found alive. That this could be open and shut. Maybe then Kelly was the one who murdered Ryan. Why else would he be alone with her in their bedroom? Finding her dead just seemed to confirm that they had been having an affair—exactly what the police had thought all along.

"But how did her body end up there?" Ella asked aloud, her thoughts giving her whiplash.

Sophia's eyes remained glued to the TV, and Nate didn't move from his spot. A small frown was on his lips, but he didn't respond.

"Who did *this*?"

38

Tiana
May 4, 2022

After Nate had left her alone in her office, Tiana didn't move for 45 minutes. For the first time in her career, she was thankful her next client hadn't shown up. She was completely incapable of functioning until suddenly, her brain forced her to.

Her cell phone rested in her hand now, and Ollie spread out like a beached whale next to her on her bed. She tried to decide what to do. Each time she unlocked her phone, she waited a few seconds before locking it again. Mental tug-of-war could not even begin to describe the bombs going off in her brain. So badly, she wanted to call Ella. To offload what Nate had burdened her with. But she had made her decision almost a week ago to protect Nate no matter what. And this was the no matter what.

Eventually, her phone vibrated, and when she saw Ella's name, she wondered for a brief second if she should even answer. But Ella hadn't been calling recently. Maybe Nate went to her and told her everything from their session. Maybe she wanted to come up with a game plan for all this. Maybe she just wanted to talk to her friend.

She swiped with a shaking finger.

"Hello?" Tiana normally answered the phone in a cheerful manner, particularly for people she loved. But it seemed like it would be a while before she could return to her old habits, particularly with Ella.

"Turn on Channel 7." Ella's frantic breathing almost obscured what she was saying.

"What?" Tiana asked, despite hearing what she had said. She reached under Ollie, who remained unbothered, in search of the remote.

"Turn on Channel 7." This time, Ella enunciated each word, letting out a quick breath between each one.

Tiana flipped on the television, expecting to see the police coming up with some trash story about Ryan and implying that he worked for the mob, or the cartel, or maybe that he was a male prostitute. Instead, she caught the tail end of the news broadcast.

"Looks like I just missed it. What was it?" Tiana asked, rolling her eyes at the possibilities running through her head.

There was a pause as Ella rustled around on the other line. "Change to Channel 12. They're playing it now."

Tiana switched channels and gasped as she read the headline.

"You think it's her?" Ella asked.

Tiana muted the TV before answering. "It would make the most sense." She bit her bottom lip, her eyes glancing over to Ollie who let out a particularly loud snore.

"They were literally searching for her. It has to be."

Tiana's eyes fell back on the television as the reporter walked along the road at the edge of the woods. In the distance, she could see a driveway. She nearly dropped the phone.

"I just don't see how it could be anybody else. And I haven't heard about any other missing persons, and I've been in and out of that police station so many times that—"

"Shut up," Tiana said, the words coming out forcefully.

"Wha—"

"Look at the driveway. Look!" Tiana was yelling now, pointing at the television with her free hand as though Ella could see.

"I'm looking."

"This is where they found the body?" Tiana hoped that Ella would tell her that it wasn't the case. Maybe it was down the road. Maybe it was just nearby.

"I think so. Why?" Irritation was beginning to develop in Ella's voice.

"Look at the mailbox." It had been hard to make out in the dark at first, but eventually, the floodlights had hit it just right, and Tiana could see the name. Painted on the metal mailbox, faded a little, clearly said "The Reeds."

Ella didn't speak, so Tiana wasn't sure if she had seen it.

"It's the cabin. They found the body near Sam's cabin."

39

Ella
May 4, 2022

Her phone bounced a little when it hit the area rug by her feet. A high-pitch squeal erupted in her ears, and her vision blurred. Before she knew it, she was on the ground, both her kids kneeling next to her.

"Mom?" Nate asked. His hand rested on her upper arm, and his fingers dug a little into her skin as he tried to get her upright.

Ella blinked a few times before she figured out she was on the floor, staring up at the ceiling. She swallowed hard and forced herself into a sitting position, with Nate's hand guiding her.

"What did Aunt T say?" Sophia asked, relaxing back on her heels.

Ella bit her bottom lip and contemplated what to say. Right now, she had no idea how the kids might be feeling. Would they be relieved Kelly Carter was found? Would they feel upset as she did? And especially, how would they feel to learn that Sam must have been involved?

"Look at the mailbox." Ella pointed at the remote, and Sophia snatched it up and hit the rewind button. For a few seconds, they all sat in silence until the light hit it just right.

"The Re—" Nate started, but stopped short, his mouth hanging open.

"What the actual fuck?" Sophia asked, her body facing away from Ella now. Ella's mouth opened reflexively to admonish her daughter, but she was right. This couldn't be happening.

"Yes. I agree" was all Ella could manage to get out. She pulled herself backwards and up onto the sectional, shaking her head once she was settled. "We can't trust anybody."

Nate looked over at his mother. "But if Sam did it, then we know who did it. We know who the killer was."

"There's no way he would *kill* Dad." There was some venom behind Sophia's words.

"Well, to be perfectly honest, sweetie, I didn't think *anybody* would ever kill your dad." Ella wished Ryan was there so badly. She wasn't sure if they could all be a unit without him. Especially as she found their support system crumbling to pieces.

"We can trust Aunt T," Nate declared confidently, sitting on the edge of the couch. Ella stared down at her hands and twirled her wedding ring. It had gotten loose the past few days since she had lost most of her appetite.

"I don't know, Nate. How can we trust anyone?" Ella looked up at her son, and his face fell.

Sophia walked over to Nate, wrapping her arms around him in a tight hug. His face was concealed, but Ella could see Sophia whispering something to him. Her heart swelled at her children coming together. They had never been particularly close, but it seemed like all of this brought them closer together. If only Ella didn't feel like pushing everyone else away.

40

Tiana
May 4, 2022

"Dad, I wish I could talk to you so badly."

In her dimly lit bedroom, Tiana choked back tears as she lay on her left side. She brushed hair out of her eyes, focusing on the picture of her and her father the last time she had visited him.

"I wish I could tell you what the hell is going on." A sob escaped her lips now. "None of this makes any sense!" Ollie lifted his head when she yelled and dragged himself closer to her on the bed, trying to lick her face, but it was just out of his reach. After a few more seconds of her pity party, she forced herself to her feet to grab some tissues. There was no sensation worse than sleeping on a wet silk pillowcase, and she wasn't about to make her situation even worse.

Before Ella's phone call, she had thought she had put all the pieces together. Nate had revealed so much, *too* much, in their session. But she had steeled herself to not reveal a peep of it. But now, it didn't make sense. How much of what Nate said was true? Did the mailbox discovery confirm the story he told? Maybe it did.

Tiana heard her phone buzzing on her dresser. After reading article after article, she had forced herself to keep her phone away when she was in bed. Doom scrolling was a very real thing, and it was awful for her sleep schedule. Her eyes widened as she saw Charlotte's name.

"Hello?" Tiana asked, her confusion clear in her voice. At first, nobody spoke on the other line, and she settled on the edge of her bed. Then, she heard it. Soft sobbing.

"I didn't know who else to call—" Charlotte's words ran together, but Tiana had a lot of experience understanding people when they cried. Tiana instinctually opened her mouth to tell her it was okay, but was interrupted. "I am so confused. Everybody is all wrapped up in this case, and I don't have anybody who will talk to me. My coworkers think *I* knew about it."

Sobs overtook Charlotte's words, and Tiana let out a slow breath as her forehead pinched together. She wasn't sure she could handle dealing with any more trauma around Ryan's death. And she hadn't even begun to tackle her own. In the back of her mind, she made a mental note to schedule an appointment with her own therapist. Would she tell her the whole truth? About Nate? She wasn't sure she could.

"Are you even listening?" Charlotte's voice had snapped back to its usual tone by the time Tiana mentally dialed back into the phone conversation.

"Yes." Tiana cleared her throat. "There's so much that I don't even know what to say." For the most part, this was true. But at the same time, she didn't really want to be Charlotte's shoulder to cry on. Honestly, Tiana found her to be a bit snobby, and it wasn't like she was taking on Ella's case pro bono. She didn't owe her anything.

"The police are still questioning him. They haven't let him out yet. And they refuse to let me see him because I'm not representing him. I mean, I can't represent him, considering the situation I'm in with Ella, but . . ."

Tiana bit her lip, ready to rage if Charlotte even suggested dropping Ella as a client. Finally, Tiana asked the question that was really on her mind. "Do *you* think he did it?"

Charlotte went silent on the line, and a sad smile spread across Tiana's face. She opened her mouth to speak, but no words came out. She didn't quite know what to think. When Charlotte didn't carry on or answer the question, Tiana pulled the phone away from her ear. Charlotte had hung up the call, and Tiana didn't care in the slightest.

Good, Tiana thought. *Let her think her ex-husband is a murderer. Maybe then she'll understand what Ella is going through.*

41

Ella
May 4, 2022

Ella glanced down at her phone as it vibrated, not wanting to answer Tiana's call. Every time she remembered Sam had a buried body on his property, she felt sick. If he wasn't stuck being questioned by the police, she was sure he would be sending frantic texts claiming that it wasn't what it looked like or that he had nothing to do with it.

But the pieces had all begun to line up. The details were still fuzzy, but the main idea was there. Sam wanted Ryan's commission so he killed him. Somehow, Kelly Carter was involved.

Ella's head played through the scene. Sam arrived at their home, prepared to murder Ryan. He was surprised to find Kelly Carter, who was likely Ryan's mistress. Classic case of wrong place, wrong time. But that part didn't sit right with Ella. Ryan cheating was unfathomable, and why had there been fentanyl in his system? Did Sam inject it? Did Kelly?

But at the end of the day, Sam had buried Kelly Carter and hoped that nobody would notice she was a part of this.

Her phone had stopped vibrating now, and she felt instant relief. If Sam killed her husband, she couldn't trust anybody. Not even Tiana.

PART TWO

42

Kelly
April 15, 2022

Creating a cleaning company was one step. Casing somebody's house wasn't that big of a leap, and just like that, she made money hand over fist.

She pushed her red hair back into a ponytail, not getting it just right until the third attempt. Part of her business was legit; it had to be. People needed reviews and references before she went into a person's home, so Kelly was strategic with her business. Nobody had caught on yet. She knew it would happen eventually, so she was ready to branch out.

It had started accidentally, just as everything seemed to for Kelly. Some might call it an unfortunate string of events, but she always landed on the upside of these tragedies. Mostly because she coordinated them. When she had been sent away to boarding school as an unruly teen, she ended up as a drug supplier for many of the kids there. Rich kids paid good money, and half the time, they couldn't even tell if what they were getting was good quality. She made sure to get good grades so nobody would suspect a thing. And by some miracle, it had worked.

Now, she was paired up with a small crew who sometimes helped her clean houses, and sometimes helped her rob them. She would give out estimates after seeing someone's home, or they would even send her pictures of every single room. It was ridiculously easy. Some people even gave her their work schedules, as if she was the most trustworthy human ever just because she was a white woman with a pretty face. Kelly had an eye for things that people wouldn't miss, and it was easy to steal when nobody was paying attention. And this was how Sam Reed found her.

When the call came in, she hadn't answered at first. Apparently, he had gotten her name from one of her suppliers, back when she used to sell. That had been too big a risk for her now that she was older. Going to jail at 18 was a lot less scary than at 29.

"I have a very specific offer."

She had almost laughed at Sam's voice. He clearly didn't spend much time in her world because he was acting like he was in *The Godfather.*

"I don't talk over the phone." Kelly rolled her eyes, waiting for him to change his mind.

"Okay, how about the gas station at—"

This time Kelly laughed. "No. I'll give you an address. It belongs to someone I know. I meet you there or nowhere at all."

She could hear him fumbling over his words on the other end.

"Okay. I guess I can—"

"Do you have a pen?"

She could hear him moving around, frantically searching for something to write with. Her eyes rolled, and for a minute, she thought about hanging up. Dumbasses like him were an occupational hazard. But at the end of the day, she wasn't really in a position to turn down work, especially before she knew what it was.

"Yes. I got one."

Kelly relayed the address to him. "Meet me there directly at ten o'clock tonight. I'll come out and get you." Of course, she wouldn't bother until ten thirty, just to test his patience. It was a bad idea to work with someone who had a quick temper. Even she had *some* standards.

43

Sam
April 15, 2022

He sat in his car staring at the house, rubbing his sweaty palms across his jeans. It was already 10:19, and he had seen no sign of the woman. She had said she would come out and get him when she was ready, but now he actively debated walking up to the house. Maybe he misremembered.

"I can't do this, I can't do this—" Sam rocked now, his eyes bloodshot. This was already too much for him to handle, but he felt like he was out of options.

Charlotte had asked for a divorce after she had found out about his gambling debts. She didn't even know about the cocaine. It was easy to keep things a secret when your schedules never lined up. Charlotte often had to work late into the night, and Sam had open houses on the weekends. Mostly, it seemed like she had wanted to separate their finances before things got too out of control, and she was right. He could get by with the apartment he had for now, but if he kept things up, he wouldn't last long. His options were limited. He could stay at the cabin and at least keep a roof over his head, but it would be impossible to do his job from there. No cell service. No Wi-Fi. No way to stay in touch with his clients. It had taken a while for him to realize that things were getting desperate; coming up with a solution had been even more difficult.

He'd be lying if he said it hadn't crossed his mind relatively easily. It made sense. It seemed simple enough. He felt bad, but not as bad as he would if he was dead broke.

There was movement at the front door of the house, and he resisted the urge to start the car and drive away. A tall, slender figure stood, and Sam shifted around in his seat, trying to get a better view. The figure didn't move off the porch, and he debated getting out. This could be a setup after all. She could have lied and sent him to a complete stranger's house.

"Screw it," he muttered under his breath as he forced the car door open. He kept his eyes focused on the porch, waiting to see if it was actually an ambush. The person lit a cigarette, and he could make out a woman's face. Relief crashed over him as he decided it must really be her, or at least, it was less likely he was about to get jumped.

"Hey, are you—" Sam stopped short when he realized he didn't know her name.

"Take off your clothes." The woman pulled the cigarette from her lips and slowly blew out a large cloud of smoke. If he had been a few steps closer, it would have surrounded his face.

"What? Um, I think I am at the wrong—" Sam started to back away. Had he accidentally arranged to meet with a prostitute instead? It wasn't like he had anything against them, but he was hoping to make money, not waste it. The woman stepped down from the porch, following him along the pathway as he backed up.

"You are a dense bastard, aren't you?" she asked, a smirk playing on her lips.

"I'm sorry—"

The woman watched him squirm for a moment longer before tossing her head back and laughing.

"Jesus Christ, you're skittish too." She tapped her cigarette against the porch railing, hot ash falling onto the cement. "I need to check you aren't wearing a wire. Take off your clothes."

Sam's forehead knitted together, and for the first time, he noticed how crisp the night air was against his exposed skin.

"Can't we go inside first?" Sam asked, gesturing toward the door. This caused the woman to step even closer, closing the distance between them so that the lit cigarette hanging from the corner of her mouth was nearly burning his cheek.

"How do I know you don't have a gun? How do I know once we go through that door you won't jump me?"

Sam didn't respond, so she leaned in closer, the cigarette singeing his five o'clock shadow.

"Huh?"

Sam stumbled backward and started to pull off his t-shirt, feeling frantic now. As much as he was terrified, he also felt his pants tighten at her aggression.

She's perfect, he thought as he stepped out of his jeans, leaving them on the pathway. When he was down to his underwear, she looked him up and down.

"Spin."

Sam tossed his arms up in the air and rotated full-circle before locking eyes with her. She stepped forward, picked up both his shirt and jeans, and ran her hand through them. She tossed his phone to the grass.

"That stays here."

Sam gave a small nod, and once more, she was closing the distance between them. He almost jumped out of his skin when she felt her hand touching his penis. It was over his underwear, but the fabric was thin. She was less efficient than a TSA agent, and Sam wondered if she enjoyed the power that she wielded over him. He was a man who needed something from her, and she loved being on top.

44

Kelly
April 15, 2022

He was small even though she could tell he was in the middle of getting hard. Kelly had seen that coming from a mile away, but all men ultimately were the same. Size didn't really matter. They were all either trying to compensate or they knew what they had and were willing to back it up.

Once she decided he was clean, she spun on her heels and walked back up the pathway, dropping the cigarette and crushing it with her black ankle boot. She moved onto the porch, her heels clicking against the cement. He didn't follow, but she carried on and opened the front door.

"Are you coming?" she asked, not looking back. She heard his footsteps scurry, most likely to pick up his clothing and to try to yank it on. She shook her head and continued to question her decision to allow this to go any further—but he had piqued her interest. He definitely wasn't her usual clientele, and he had passed the patience test, mostly.

The house belonged to one of the guys on her cleaning crew, but he never did any of the actual cleaning. He was an expert at assessing the value of collectibles, and he was smart enough to skip over ones that people would miss. She could unleash him on a basement or attic, and within an hour, he would have found anything worth having. He didn't live a lavish lifestyle. Instead, he lived in a one-story, beat-down home, with stained shag carpeting and wood paneling, and unsurprisingly, his own collectibles were not on display.

Kelly settled in a recliner that was the color of cat vomit and crossed her legs.

The man stood awkwardly in the center of the room before perching on the edge of the loveseat, his discomfort still obvious. He had forgotten to zip his fly when he had put his pants back on.

"I'm Kelly. You're Sam Reed?" Kelly asked, holding his brown wallet in her hand.

He blinked, his mild confusion evolving into something much larger.

"Yeah," he choked out. She sighed and tossed his wallet back across the room. He failed to catch it, and he leaned down to pluck it off the floor. He held it in his hand, rubbing his thumb back and forth across the leather.

"So what's the job?"

"I—" She could see him swallow hard and shake his head slightly. "I need someone dead."

The corner of Kelly's mouth turned upward, and she leaned back in the recliner, rocking slightly.

"Who?" She was intrigued. It wasn't every day that someone asked her to do that. She had only done it once before—when a crew member had crossed her. Greg. His name should have tipped her off, but she ignored it. She had never met a trustworthy man named *Greg*. At the end of the day, she had made an example of him. It was a smart business decision. She hadn't made a habit of it.

"Ryan Thomas."

Ella shrugged. "And who is the lucky bastard to you?"

"A coworker," Sam shrugged, but she saw his eyes look away from her just for a split second.

"And?" Her voice was stern, her eyes narrowing on him.

"My friend."

Kelly shook her head. "What the fuck, dude? Why?" The more she heard, the less she liked this. But something about him kept her pushing forward despite the pull of her intuition telling her to stop.

"I work in real estate. If he dies, I get his caseload. And he has a major case—"

"And a huge commission," Kelly finished, nodding along. "How big?"

"I'm not sure exactly, but it could be close to six digits."

Kelly's eyebrows raised, but she quickly forced them back down. Her poker face had slipped for just a second. "I get half."

Sam shook his head. "I can't give up that much. I have some debts to settle, and it won't stretch far enough. It has to be *worth* it."

Kelly laughed, her curls swaying on her shoulders. "If it's six digits, I get 50 grand. I'll call it a day."

"And if it's not six digits?" Sam asked. Kelly was staring down at her almond-shaped fingernails and watched the dim light of the room bounce off the red paint.

"Then I guess it wasn't worth it, huh?"

45

Sam
April 15, 2022

A switch had flipped in Sam by the time he had sat down inside the house. He had a pretty good idea of what had gotten his adrenaline running, and his paranoia and doubt were gone now. He didn't allow himself to show it on the surface—it was a good disguise for the sake of this meeting. She didn't need to know him. In fact, it was better she didn't.

"So how does this work then?" Sam asked, rubbing his palms against his jeans again, even though the sweat from earlier had completely dried up. He glanced down at his pants and noticed the fly was down, but he decided to leave it. "Do we make a blood oath or something?" He offered a small chuckle, but she didn't join him.

"Obviously, there's no paperwork. But I have your word that when this is over, I get the majority share.

For the time being, I need collateral. Maybe your car?" she asked, an eyebrow raised.

"I need it to get to work. It'd be suspicious if I didn't have a car all the sudden." Her pushiness made him feel disgusted. Even though he was doing a horrible thing, possibly one of the worst things you could do to a person, he still felt like she was a cockroach in society.

"Then you better find a way to get me 10,000 dollars."

Sam frowned and shook his head slowly. "If I had that much money, this conversation wouldn't even be happening." His frustration was bubbling under the surface, one of the veins in his forehead was beginning to bulge, but he knew it wasn't visible to Kelly in the dim light of the room.

"Fine. 5,000, final offer."

Sam blew out a breath and shook his head. "I can try to pull it together."

"You better." Kelly stood up and moved over to him. He hated how she loomed over him with her holier-than-thou attitude. "And if you don't get me my cut, after this is all done"—her eyebrows knit together in a way Sam found rather unflattering—"I will do the same damn thing to you. Except it will be slow. You'll wish you were dead by the time I'm done with you."

It took everything in Sam not to laugh in her face. Instead, he bobbed his head up and down like a drinking bird. "Understood." His voice accidentally cracked when he spoke. It was too perfect.

"Now get the hell out of here."

Sam had to slip around her as he rose from the loveseat.

"When will it happen?" he asked.

"I'll do some surveillance and get back to you. I might need your help coordinating something."

"I figured someone like you would be full service, without needing any help." Sam's mask slipped for just a moment, and he fumbled to bring himself back under control.

"Everybody needs help." She shrugged. "Otherwise, you wouldn't be here." Kelly winked and walked toward the front door, pushing it open for him. Sam kept his head down as he headed out the door, finally zipping his fly once he was on the porch. The door swung shut behind him, and he exhaled slowly. His nerves were on fire, but in the way that he chased on the daily. He settled behind the wheel of his car and checked his wallet. She hadn't taken any cash, and he had just enough to throw away. His car roared to life, and he turned onto the road in the opposite direction he had come, heading straight for the casino.

46

Kelly
April 15, 2022

Kelly watched through the front door as Sam disappeared down the street. There was still doubt tugging on the edges of her mind, but she shook it off and headed to a back bedroom.

The dark room had several large surveillance screens on it, and a lanky figure sat at the helm of a computer. The man gave Kelly a quick smile, revealing a missing canine tooth in the upper right. His head was shaved, and a patchy beard was growing.

"Did you get all that?" Kelly asked, settling herself on the bed and leaning forward with her elbows resting on her knees.

"Every word," Tony said, leaning back in the chair. He was playing the stream back now. Kelly watched herself toss the wallet across the room. The videos always made for a very convincing insurance policy. It would be easy enough for Tony to edit Kelly out of the video entirely, leaving Sam to incriminate himself. It also worked well if anybody on her crew ever needed legal immunity. Even though murder for hire was new to her, she wasn't a rookie. And she had a sneaking suspicion that Sam might fold under the pressure.

"What do you think of him?" Kelly leaned away from the screen, pulled off her boots, and massaged the heel of her right foot.

"Honestly, I'm not sure. He made a comment at the end that spooked me a little."

Kelly nodded. "You're just insulted he thinks we are running a minor-league operation here." She playfully hit his shoulder. "Besides, he was probably just flirting."

"I mean when a guy spends enough time with you, it's hard not to." Tony grinned and Kelly shook her head, a smile playing on her lips. Their relationship was good-natured; but she'd given herself a rule to never get into relationships with clients or colleagues, which was more than a lot of people with real jobs did.

"Let's get Kyle and Ricky to start watching him." She was standing now, grabbing a small, chestnut-brown purse from the bed. Tony nodded eagerly. She paused for a second, turning around before she was out the door. "Both of them, Tony."

47

Sam
April 16, 2022

"This is the start of something great, I'll tell you that."
Ryan handed Sam a beer he had just cracked open.
Together, they were standing in his garage, the door
open and letting in a mild spring breeze. Sam tipped
the bottle up to his lips and drank eagerly.

"It definitely could be," Sam said, nodding his head,
and Ryan led him through the back door of the garage
and out to the backyard. The barbeque was going, ribs
already cooking. The kids were probably just now
waking up for the day. Ella was inside making up some
broccoli salad.

Ryan turned around and walked up the porch steps
backward, gesturing to Sam with his beer.

"Don't be a pessimist! Or a realist, I guess," Ryan
decided, shaking his head slightly.

Sam didn't want to build up doubt inside his friend,
but his conversation with Kelly Carter was fresh in his

head. It was the start of something great, just not for Ryan.

"So, what are you going to do?" Sam asked, settling down into one of the patio chairs. The cushion was firm, barely moving as he put his full weight on it. He slouched. His head was still pounding a bit from the night before. He couldn't remember all that had happened, but he woke up on a hotel-room bed. The covers had never even been pulled back.

"Obviously, I'm going to win them over as a client." Ryan opened the lid to the grill and peeked inside before nodding to himself. He turned around, his full attention on Sam now. "And then I'm going to pay for Sophia's college."

Sam grinned at the suggestion, but inside he cringed. It was grossly unfair to be stealing from Sophia, a girl with such a promising future.

"Not Nate's?" he asked, an eyebrow raised. Both men dissolved into laughter a moment later. It wasn't that Nate wasn't smart. It was that he didn't apply himself. And although he had never once mentioned what his plans were after graduation in a year and a half, none of them for a moment thought more school was in the cards.

"But just college? That's boring." Sam was already halfway done with his beer. He began playing with the label on the bottle, hoping it would slow him down.

"Well, I was thinking about doing something special for Ella. Maybe a trip. Some renovations around the house if the money goes that far."

Sam hadn't known exactly how much money the commission could be, but it sounded like Ryan had a pretty good idea. And if it was big enough that he was thinking about these things, it was probably more than

Sam originally suspected. His brain jump started and he blinked a few times.

"Hey, what about getting somebody to help clean up around the house? I know a lady." Sam regretted the words as soon as he said them. It wasn't something he and Kelly had agreed on, but it seemed like a good opportunity. The perfect opportunity, really.

"What are you saying about my house?" Ryan jested. "Yeah, that could be a great idea. Ella's so busy with the kids and work, I bet she would love that. Send me her number."

"Um, she can be weird about giving out her number." Sam was stumbling over his words now, but an idea popped into place just in time. "She used to have a really abusive boyfriend, and so she doesn't put her name and number out there. That's part of what makes her business so difficult to promote—she only uses word of mouth." Sam put his beer to his lips again, feeling rather proud of his response.

"Oh, shit." Ryan nodded and ran a hand through his hair. "Yeah, I guess you can give her my number instead?"

Sam nodded. "Will do. I'm sure she'll be happy to get in touch."

48

Kelly
April 18, 2022

"It's going to be so easy. I'm going to tell you when he will be home alone, and all you have to do is show up and get the job done."

Kelly rolled her eyes and readjusted her position in her car. They were parked side by side at a local park. Enough of a coincidence that nobody would ever suspect. Sam was looking eagerly over at her, despite her telling him not to make eye contact. "It will be the easiest job you've ever had. He'll let you right in the front door!"

Kelly wanted to scream. Of course, it would be easy. She hadn't made a cleaning company her front without cause.

"And what then?" she asked, her annoyance edging slightly into her voice. Setting this up *was not* his part in this. She didn't like being told how to do these things.

"I was thinking drugs," Sam offered, turning his head away now, glancing around at a few kids playing on the equipment.

"An overdose?" she asked. She wondered if Sam knew a single thing about drugs, but she reminded herself that he had to get in contact with her somehow, and it definitely wasn't from the yellow pages.

"Or something laced with something else?" Sam glanced over at her, but she had no real reaction.

"I guess that works. Is he a user already?" Kelly asked. She figured the answer was no, but it was an important question. If he had a potential tolerance to certain substances, they may only send him on a serious trip rather than a permanent vacation.

"No. Definitely not." Sam shook his head. "Probably never even touched pot."

Kelly nodded. "Okay. Should be easy then."

"We have to move soon. If they get too far along in the signing process—"

Kelly figured he had forgotten who he was talking to. She didn't care one bit about all of that, as long as she got her money.

"And?" Kelly asked, holding out her hand, palm open.

Sam bit his bottom lip before reaching into the glove box of his car. He pulled out a Walmart bag and passed it over quickly, looking side to side. Kelly wanted to slap him with the cash. He was making himself look so obvious that she half thought it was a setup. The only saving grace was that cops wouldn't be so foolish. She pulled open the bag on her lap, taking a quick glance. She couldn't tell if it was quite the amount they agreed on, but it was enough for now.

Kelly turned her key in the ignition. "Tell me when."

She rolled up her window and slipped her sunglasses up properly over her eyes. She drove off before Sam had a chance to say anything else.

49

Sam
April 25, 2022

"Yeah, I know it's boring, but I think we both have to go tonight." Sam shrugged, leaning back in his office chair. Ryan was perched in the chair across from him, his left knee bent, ankle resting on his right knee.

"Part of the job, I guess." Ryan frowned, running his hand through his styled brown hair and messing it up accidentally. "If Geller is supposed to be there, I should go home and change." Ryan stopped just short of wiping the mousse from his hands on his dress pants.

"Navy suit?" Sam asked, the corner of his mouth upturned.

Ryan chuckled and stood up. "You know it. I'll just run home after lunch." He was halfway out the door of Sam's office. "Guess I better start doing my actual job."

Sam nodded and looked down at his own desk as Ryan left. He could feel the sweat traveling down the center of his back. This was going to be harder than he thought, but desperate times called for desperate measures. He pulled out his phone and sent a text before leaning back in his chair and wiping his forehead with a tissue. Panic was already swelling in him, and nothing had even happened yet.

There was an intense tug-of-war going on in his head. One side told him that what he was doing was unforgivable; meanwhile, the other side didn't care in the slightest. If he had to go after Ryan's family, he would. It didn't matter the cost—he had to get himself out of this situation, regardless.

50

Kelly
April 25, 2022

"Yes, hello. My name is Alicia. Sam Reed gave me your info and told me that you might be interested in some cleaning services?" Kelly's voice went up an octave once Ryan had answered. Her customer service voice. It was quite convincing.

"Oh, hi, Alicia!" Ryan chirped.

She could tell he was distracted. From her parking spot across the street, she could barely make out him fumbling to get into his car while holding his phone in one hand and his bag in the other.

"I'd love the chance to come over and give you a quote." Kelly forced herself to hold back, not wanting to sound too eager.

"That would be awesome. What's your availability?" His car door slammed after he finished his question.

"Well—" she chuckled slightly, something she had practiced earlier that day "—I am actually available for the next hour if we could make that work. Otherwise, I could come by later in the week."

"Oh," he paused, clearly surprised by her offer. She had hoped her practice had paid off. She had to make it seem like the world's biggest coincidence. It should look strange rather than inconvenient and pushy. "I guess that works."

"If not, we can—" she was backpedaling now, tuning in to his discomfort.

"No, now is totally fine," Ryan insisted, suddenly making it seem like he had been the one to suggest it.

A smile crept onto Kelly's lips, and she watched herself in the car visor's mirror. Her face looked foreign without the makeup she normally painted on. She particularly focused in on her lips, how they were barely pink, and the bandana covering most of her hair. She certainly looked the part. And god, she hated it.

"Great. Could you text me the address?" she asked, even though she knew damn well what it was and how to get there with three different routes.

"I'll do that right now. See you soon." Ryan hung up and sent the text before starting his car and pulling out of the parking lot. She waited a few minutes before following, hoping to catch him just as he entered the house. Before pulling away, she checked her purse one final time, making sure the needle was prepped and ready.

"Let's go," she murmured, giving herself one last look in the mirror. Even without all the makeup, there was a faint glimmer in her eye that she recognized. She held onto that and drove after Ryan Thomas one last time.

51

Sam
April 25, 2022

He had stationed himself a few houses down and across the street from the Thomas home. His car wouldn't look out of place, especially considering Ryan had the exact same one, but he didn't want anyone to see him watching the house. That was the kind of thing people called the cops for. But it was daylight, and people were less skittish. The sky had darkened with storm clouds, and the turmoil of it made Sam feel at ease.

A few minutes ago, he had watched Ryan open the door for Kelly and her follow him in, carrying just her purse. She looked entirely different than she had when he had met her the previous two times. If anything, he had to give her credit for getting into character quite well.

His leg tapped impatiently as he sat.

"How long is she going to wait?" Sam mumbled, trying to get a glimpse of anything through the windows of the house. He was able to faintly make out them walking into a few of the rooms, her checking out the house properly as if she was truly giving him an estimate.

Sam reached over and opened his glove box, double-checking to make sure everything he needed was there. Two needles, just in case, as well as a gun he had bought off the street when he started taking money from loan sharks. When he did that, he knew it would only be a matter of time before they started seeking him out. He tucked the gun into the front of his pants and grabbed both needles, planning to follow Kelly into the house. That hadn't been part of her plan, but it was always his. Nobody could go after your money if they were dead, after all.

Movement caught the corner of his eye and his head flicked back up to the house. He could make out Nate and Sophia heading up the pathway to the house. They were home early from school.

"Fuck. Fuck." He scrambled to pull his burner phone out of his pocket, hoping to send an SOS text to Kelly. His finger hovered over the unlock key as he got a text from Kelly.

Just finishing up now.

His stomach dropped.

"No. No," he mumbled over and over again, his voice with the edge of a scream on it. Sam watched the front door open and close. For a moment, the only sound was his heavy breathing.

"It's fine," he lied. Kelly could slip out the back. The plan could still work.

Then, he heard it. A gunshot rang out, then another. He frantically looked from house to house surrounding him, waiting for people to hover in the windows of their homes. For them to come out to their front lawns, cell phones pressed against their ears, telling a dispatcher their location. But nobody came. There was movement in a few windows, but of course, there was nothing to see except Sam, who had pushed his seat back and nearly lay down to avoid being spotted.

"I'm sorry, kids," he whispered after a minute, wetness filling the rims of his eyes. But no real tears came. He didn't want them to die, but they shouldn't have gotten home so damn early. The phone Kelly had given him didn't light up with another message, and he figured she must be panicking too. She just killed two kids. Two more people than she was planning on. His stomach flipped, and for just a minute, he felt deep regret. But it was just for a moment. Then he drove away.

52

Ella
May 5, 2022

She sat in the waiting area, her legs crossed, her hair pin straight. She was due for a trim. The blonde locks were getting a little too long for her liking, but she hadn't had the time, of course. But she had taken the time this morning to meticulously get ready. To put on one of the outfits she would use for Ryan's work Christmas parties. It felt good to cover up the redness on her face and the bags under her eyes. For the first time since the murder, she even put on mascara.

"Mrs. Thomas." Dave Clemens appeared at the entryway to the long hallway behind him. The door had a lock system on it that you needed a key card to access.

Ella unfolded her legs and rose and felt a little wobbly on her heels as she stood, but by the time she had closed the distance between them, her stride was confident.

Clemens turned around as the metal door swung shut behind them. The hallway chilled Ella's skin, and her eyes slowly adjusted to the low lighting.

"Ella, I really do not think this is a good idea."

Ella shrugged and held her hands together in front of her, her knuckles turning white as she clutched her purse.

"I don't really give a shit what you think, Dave."

Her opinion of the man had tanked when Sam was arrested for the murder. He had twisted her mind around so much that she thought her late husband was a drug-addicted cheater. At the very least, she would be grateful if he had been the one to find Kelly's body, but that had been the search-and-rescue party, primarily thanks to a pack of search dogs. Ella laughed a little bit every time she thought about the fact that the police dogs were better detectives than Clemens.

"Let me be clear: I am *only* doing this because I feel guilty about how I treated you. And your kids. Mostly your kids." His eyes softened at the mention of Nate and Sophia. Ella imagined that he was the type of man who had his own kids, or at least nieces and nephews. She could feel genuine sympathy radiating off him. "And it might help the case," he tacked on. It seemed like an afterthought, like he was justifying what was by all accounts a bad decision.

"And I am not supposed to breathe a word of this to Charlotte. I know." Ella rolled her eyes and swallowed hard. She was putting on a good show, but really, she could feel hot bile rising at the bottom of her esophagus.

"Fine." Clemens turned back around and headed deeper down the hallway before making a left turn and stopping. Behind the glass, she smiled a bit when she saw Sam in the orange jumpsuit. It made her feel vindicated that he was in there, but those feelings quickly faded to anger and despair. He took away her husband. He took away her children's father. He took *everything* away from her.

"I can give you five minutes. That's all." Clemens's voice drew her back into the moment. She nodded and he scanned his key card before opening the door.

"That's all I need." Ella stepped around Clemens and through the door. Sam looked up, and his eyes lit up.

"Ella. Oh my god. I'm so relieved to see you." He stayed in the chair, and Ella quickly realized his wrists were cuffed and hooked to the table. She moved over to the table, pulled the chair back, and sat down a whole foot away from the table.

"How are they treating you?" Ella surprised herself by asking that question. Her mind didn't really care in the slightest how he was treated, unless the answer was 'well.' In that case, she cared a lot.

"I hate it here. It's awful. And the cops are so pissed at me. They think I'm some killer pulling the wool over their eyes. But I didn't do it, I swear." Sam's eyes were frantic, searching her face. She gave up nothing.

"Why should we believe that?" Ella's voice was flat, and her face remained neutral. It was like she was taking a lie detector test and was trying her best not to set off any alarm bells.

"I have no idea who that woman is. Never met her in my life. Somebody put her there. Somebody set me up."

Ella resisted the urge to roll her eyes again. She hated men, especially now that Ryan was gone. He was apparently the only decent one in the entire country.

"Who would do that?" She pretended to humor him, but really, she was hoping he would accidentally get caught in his own lie. She didn't have to look behind her to know that Clemens was recording this interaction. She told herself that earlier he was just acting. He didn't feel guilty. The real reason he agreed to this was probably to get more evidence on Sam.

"I don't—" Sam paused, and for a minute, Ella felt like she could see behind the mask. He let out a sigh. "To be honest, I owed some people a lot of money."

Ella felt the breath leak out of her lungs. There it was. He admitted it was all about the money. The commission. Rage bubbled in her stomach.

"They must have done this. It was a warning. I don't know if they wanted me to end up in jail or just scare me by killing Ryan. I don't know, Ella. I really just don't know—"

Ella rose back up to her feet and hiked her purse onto her shoulder. She could feel Clemens's eyes burning a hole through the back of her head as he watched on the other side of the glass.

"I am so sorry. I never meant for all this to happen."

Ella wondered if that part was even the slightest bit true.

"Shut up." The words were quiet and soft and didn't quite catch Sam's attention.

"How are the kids holding up? Do they really think I did this?" he asked, and a shiver went up Ella's back. She stared down at him, her eyebrows woven together.

"I don't think you have a right to ask me about my children." Her voice wavered a little now, and she struggled to not begin shaking.

"Why don't you ask Nate if he thinks I did this, huh? Why don't you ask him what really—"

The sound that Ella's open palm made when it hit Sam's face was louder than she expected. When her hand pulled away, she was surprised at how much it stung and how red his face was.

Sam's mouth hung open, the words he was going to say frozen in his mouth. Ella pulled her purse up over her shoulder and headed for the door, which Clemens had already yanked open. Ella glanced at his face, noticing the anger on it but not apologizing. When the door shut behind her, she headed back down the hall and toward the exit.

"Ella. Ella!" Clemens nearly shouted after her.

She paused, turned halfway, and regarded him.

"What the hell?"

Ella shrugged and turned back around. Her mind wondered if Clemens was second-guessing himself now. Did he think that maybe Sam was actually innocent, and that Nate was responsible? The words had stung as Sam had said them, not because she thought they were untrue, but because she had trusted him with her own suspicions. At that point, she didn't have enough information. And the money at play changed things completely. She knew now that she was wrong to even think Nate played a part. Clearly, it was Sam all along.

53

Tiana
May 5, 2022

Her fingernails were bit down so short they were almost bleeding. She sat in her office with her laptop, reading every news article she could get her hands onto regarding Sam's arrest. Even after she had voraciously read them all, she went back, meticulously looking for something, anything, that confirmed her doubts.

Her phone rang on the coffee table and she leaned forward to grab it.

Ella.

She let out a slow breath and unlocked her phone, preparing herself to lie.

"Hey, how are you holding up?" Tiana asked, trying to keep her voice casual.

"I just slapped Sam Reed."

Tiana leaned forward, her eyebrows rising. "You did what?" Clearly, she hadn't heard her correctly. Sam was in jail.

"I went down to the police station and saw him. Clemens felt guilty or whatever and let me. And—" Ella sniffed as though she was crying. Tiana frowned, her stomach doing flips. She could feel what was coming. "He said that Nate had something to do with it all."

There it was. Alarm bells screeched in Tiana's head. This was the moment she had been dreading. She hadn't really decided whether she would tell the truth or not. Or, at least, parts of the truth that Nate had told her. *If* they were true. Tiana felt like she was going to be sick, and she couldn't imagine how Ella was feeling. Ella sniffed a few more times before Tiana realized she was supposed to say something.

"What?" she asked, but it felt forced, as if she was pretending she hadn't heard her. "Why would he say something like that?"

"Because I told him I thought he might!" Ella burst into sobs now, and Tiana sat up straight, using her free hand to pull her curls away from her face.

"What?" It wasn't forced this time. She had never imagined that Ella might suspect Nate of anything. Ryan was *his* father. After a moment, Ella was able to regulate her breathing again.

"He's been acting strange ever since it happened. It's weird." Ella paused. "It sounds ridiculous hearing myself say it now."

Tiana wanted so badly to tell her friend that yes, it sounded completely wild that Nate had done something that day. But at the same time—

"He has been very kind," Tiana agreed. "But he's usually nice to me. Maybe he just knows you need the support." It wasn't totally incorrect.

A knock sounded on Tiana's door and she rose to her feet. "Somebody's here. Hold on."

Tiana peeked out the front window to see Clemens standing on her walkway. He must have left the station immediately after Ella did.

"Shit. I have to go. I'm sorry. We can talk more later," Tiana rushed the words out, hanging up before Ella could put a response together. Ollie was barking upstairs at the sound of the front door, and she didn't bother telling him to be quiet. She straightened out her blush-rose blouse and opened the door.

"Ms. Hill," Clemens said, a respectful smile spreading across his lips. Tiana didn't return it.

"Detective Clemens." Tiana resisted the urge to step back and invite him into her office. Instead, she held her ground, holding onto the doorknob tightly.

"May I come in?" he asked, a foot ready to step inside.

"I would rather you didn't." Tiana's pulse steadily increased until she could hear her blood whooshing in her ears. She would be lying if she said she wasn't a little afraid of cops. And not giving them what they wanted was terrifying.

"Okay. I am here to claim any records from sessions you provided to Nate Thomas."

Sweat ran down her spine, and her knees felt like they might give out, but she didn't let it show. He had heard what Sam said about Nate, and he decided to pursue the lead. Immediately.

"Do you have a warrant?" she asked, tilting her head slightly to the right.

Clemens let out a small laugh. Tiana felt her grip tighten even more on the doorknob. He had thought she would just hand them over with no questions.

"You don't have to make this difficult. I just have to make a few phone calls, and I will have a warrant. So if you just give them to me, then we both don't have to waste our time with this little song and dance."

"Detective Clemens, I will not violate patient confidentiality. I cannot even confirm that he has received any amount of therapy from me. So please, go right ahead and waste our time."

They both stood in silence while Tiana wondered if she could muster up the strength to shut the door on him.

"Fair enough." Clemens pulled his phone out of his pocket and turned around to head back to his car, which was parked in front of her driveway. She couldn't leave if he stayed there. She had never considered herself claustrophobic, but she imagined it would feel something like this.

She swung the door shut and let out a slow breath. This was only the beginning.

54

Sophia
April 25, 2022

"May I go to the guidance counselor?" Sophia whispered to her teacher.

Mr. Fredericks looked at her through his thick-framed glasses. Sophia never asked to leave class, not even to go to the bathroom. She had trained herself just to do that in between classes or during lunch.

"Fine," Mr. Fredericks grumbled, and he jotted down a pass for her.

"Thank you." She quickly gathered up her belongings before he could change his mind, and she headed out the door. She only made it about halfway down the stairwell when the panic attack hit. Her body was being crushed in a vise, and she collapsed into the corner of the stairwell landing. Her water bottle clattered to the ground and rolled a few times before hitting the opposite wall.

She had failed the test. She had *never* failed a test in her life. Not even a spelling test in elementary school. Her upper body rocked with her sobs, and she found herself alone in her own world. The brick walls around her were closing in, and the cool floor tiles only made her feel clammy. Even though she was only a sophomore, colleges would be paying attention, and she had always had her eyes on somewhere Ivy League. But Algebra 2 just didn't make any sense to her. She would study for hours and go into the test feeling confident, only to get slapped in the face when the grade came back. Mr. Fredericks was useless at teaching math, and she was drowning.

In reality, of course, she was still passing the class. It was one test. But a grade in the lower 80s was enough to bring down her GPA and pull her away from the top 5 percent of her highly competitive class.

Her lungs struggled to pull in air, and she began to get even more panicked. She'd never had one so bad before. In fact, after feeling this, she wasn't sure if she had ever truly had a panic attack.

"Sophia?"

She heard her name being called, but she felt like she was underwater. She was scared to look and see who was talking to her. A hand touched her shoulder, and she jerked away, looking up now.

Nate stood over her, genuine concern painted on his face.

Sophia didn't answer, but rubbed her face against the long sleeves of her shirt. Both came away soaked and snot coated.

"Where are you supposed to be?" Nate asked, kneeling down next to his sister. He reached over, grabbed her water bottle, and handed it to her. "Take a sip."

Sophia listened, unscrewing the lid while she processed her older brother in front of her. She took a small sip of water before feeling confident enough to take a longer one. She ended up sputtering, choking on the last bit she swallowed. Nate patted her back as though it would help. His touch was foreign to her, and although she didn't have anything particularly against her brother, she hated to be touched. She shrugged slightly away.

"Math," Sophia answered. "That dumbass Fredericks can't teach to save his damn life."

Nate nodded. "I've heard bad things about him." He hadn't taken the higher-level math classes when he was younger, so he was only in Algebra 2 despite being a grade above her.

The two sat in silence for a while, Sophia still catching her breath.

"Where did you tell him you were going?" Nate asked, gesturing toward her pass.

"The counselor."

Nate smiled.

"Let's go home."

"What?" Sophia shook her head and started to stand up.

"Fredericks is not going to check if you ever showed up there. It's the last period of the day. Let's just leave."

Sophia wondered how many times her brother had done this. He always ended up getting home before her, but she had assumed he just walked faster. His legs were quite a bit longer than hers. But now, it made sense. He was leaving early. All the time.

"We'll get in trouble."

Nate shook his head. "You won't. I might," he admitted, "but I don't really care. And to be honest, my teacher probably hasn't even realized how long I've been gone."

Standing next to her brother, she felt a little giddy. Bad behavior was not something in her social repertoire. Even if she thought the majority of the planet was full of idiots, she kept her mouth shut and her head down. It would take a long time, but eventually, she would find herself in a position of power. If she was being honest, that was what she wanted the most. Skipping school didn't fit into the *plan*, but it did seem like a small taste of what her future could be like.

"I mean, I guess we can."

"Definitely. And guess what, I'll even go one step further. If you get in trouble, I'll take the fall for it. I'll tell them that I made you. Kidnapped you or something."

Sophia let out a laugh that quickly turned into a snort. "Fine." She pulled her Vera Bradley backpack over her shoulders and wiped her tears once more.

"Let's go." Nate held out his arm as though he was going to escort her. She shook her head and stepped ahead of him, heading for the exit at the bottom of the stairwell.

55

Nate
April 25, 2022

"How often do you do this?" Sophia asked as she strolled next to him on the sidewalk. There were a few strong gusts of wind, but the rain hadn't started yet.

"Few times a month." Nate shrugged. It was probably more like once or twice a week, but his sister didn't need to know that. He wondered if maybe he was doing something wrong by helping her cut class. The last thing he wanted was to send her down the wrong path.

"And you don't get in trouble?" Sophia asked, disbelief painted on her face.

"Sometimes I do. Depends on the teacher. Sometimes they're just happy to not have me in the room."

"What?" Sophia barked, her eyebrows raised. "You cause that much trouble? Jesus Christ, Nate. You shouldn't be like that to teachers. They don't deserve that. Except for Fredericks. He can burn in hell."

"Whoa there, tiger. It's nothing like that. They just have a lot of kids in the room at a time. It's not like the AP classes where there are only like twenty kids in a class. These rooms are packed. There's no room to breathe most of the time. Sometimes, teachers just don't care because I get the work done eventually." Nate paused. "Okay, I get the work done that I need to pass."

Sophia chuckled, and Nate felt a little satisfied with himself for being able to cheer her up so much.

"My turn to ask you a question." Nate kicked a rock on the sidewalk, and it rolled in front of Sophia, who kicked it forward again. "Why do you care so much?"

Sophia's face contorted for a moment, and Nate stumbled.

"I don't mean it like that. I just—"

"No, it's fine. I do care more than most people. I just have been working so hard all this time, and I really don't know why. What's the point if some asshole like Fredericks comes along and tanks my perfect record just because he's incompetent at his job? Mom and Dad work pretty hard, right? And they've never really caught a break. I don't want my life to be like that. I don't want to wake up each day, exhausted, to go to work for some guy that I hate. That sounds like absolute hell."

Nate nodded. He had often thought about how the rest of life would be, and his parents had told him that he was throwing his life away with the decisions he was making. Half the time, Nate didn't care because it didn't really matter to him if he made it that far. The rest of the time, he felt like a piece of shit for letting the people around him down. The feeling was so crippling that he couldn't force himself to change. A self-fulfilling prophecy.

"So, I want to be better off than them. That's why I work so hard. And why I hate Fredericks so damn much." A stray tear fell down his sister's cheek, and he debated reaching out and hugging her. But their relationship wasn't like that, so he just kept walking beside her.

Their house was coming into sight down the road, and Nate wished for a moment this could last longer. He wanted to be able to support his sister more, but he could feel the moment slipping through his fingers.

"Screw Fredericks. You're gonna do great things anyway." Nate could feel himself getting choked up, but Sophia playfully shoved him and he laughed instead.

"Gross. Don't talk about me like that." Her lip was curled up in fake disgust, and he smiled.

They were coming up from the front walkway now, and he reached into his pocket for his key.

"When we get in, I'm going to revise my English essay."

"No rest for the wick—" Nate stopped short. The doorknob turned in his hand without any resistance from the lock. "It's open."

He turned to regard Sophia, an eyebrow raised. She shrugged.

"Dad must have forgotten." Sophia trudged into the house ahead of him without another word.

56

Tiana
May 4, 2022

"Then let me tell you what really happened."

Tiana's stomach lurched when Nate said that. She leaned back in her chair because she feared for a moment that she might pass out.

"I got home early." Nate paused, and then shook his head, a small smile on his lips. "I shouldn't have been home yet. I skipped class.

"When I walked in the front door, everything seemed normal. I went into the kitchen to grab a snack. But just as I opened the pantry door, I heard a noise upstairs. Nobody else was supposed to be home. I *wasn't* supposed to be home. I went upstairs, and I saw it. I'm not really sure what happened, but my dad was on the bed. His gun was on the bed next to him, and when I walked farther into the room, I stepped on something. A needle. There was blood everywhere." He let out a slow breath.

Tiana crossed and uncrossed her legs, struggling to stay still.

"It was like I was in a trance. I couldn't stop myself. I just kept going farther into the room. I got around to the side of the bed, and a woman was there."

Tiana frowned. "Kelly Carter?"

"I guess. I'd never seen her before. All I knew was she was dead. Shot. And my dad had a gun next to him. And I just—I didn't know what to do. I just decided to hide her. I couldn't let my dad be found like that. Drugs? Cheating on my mom? It would *break* my mom." He was stumbling over his words, struggling to keep them straight.

"So you hid her."

Nate nodded, biting his bottom lip. "I keep thinking about how heavy she was. She was so skinny, but I could barely hold her up. I—I found a tarp in the garage so that it wouldn't get blood all over the house. I took her in my dad's car and buried her. And I hoped like hell that nobody would notice.

"I realize how absurd that sounds now, but I wasn't thinking straight. It was like my mind just went blank, and my body was moving, but I wasn't telling it to do things. It *just* did them. I pretended to get home right when Sophia did. She always stays late after school, tutoring someone or getting a teacher to look over something. Clubs. Whatever. And then . . ." Nate's voice broke now, and tears fell down his face. Tiana's heart clenched and she wanted to hold him, but her mind was still caught up on everything he was offloading on her. "I set Sophia up to find him. I didn't think there was any other way.

"I just keep thinking about her face afterwards. How she looked at me. I can't get rid of it."

He covered his face with his hands, and Tiana nodded.

"Of course. That must be so hard to live with."

Nate nodded. Neither of them spoke. Nate wiped his tears on the sleeve of his hoodie, even though tissues sat on the coffee table in front of them. Normally, Tiana would lean forward and offer them, but she found herself glued to the spot.

"Thanks for letting me get all that out," Nate murmured as he collected himself.

"Clearly, that's what I'm here for."

Nate gave her a sad smile, and she did hurt for him. Despite it all. He was just trying to protect his mother.

"I'm going to head out now. I do feel a little better." The session was only halfway over, but there was no way she would ask him to stay.

"Good. I'm glad. Tell your mom I said hi."

Nate rose to his feet, but Tiana stayed in place, running her right thumb over the back of her left hand. When he saw she wasn't getting up, he left.

Tiana stared at the door with one thought on her mind. He was lying. And she knew it.

57

Ella
May 6, 2022

"He had his arraignment hearing today," Charlotte droned on through the phone.

Ella imagined her pinching the bridge of her nose between her thumb and pointer finger. Somehow, the roles had flipped between them. Charlotte was spilling her life out on the table, and Ella just had to listen in case she happened to share something relevant. She had waited for Nate's name to come up, but Charlotte hadn't mentioned it once. It seemed like they weren't planning on bringing him in for questioning.

"That's where they decide on bail, right?" Ella asked, her attention finally tuning into what was being said. She was sitting in the parking lot at work. She hadn't felt quite ready to go back to work, and luckily, her boss was willing to let her do some of the medical billing from home. She sat with the files in her lap, staring straight out the windshield, listening as carefully as she could to Charlotte.

"Yes."

"And?"

"He's out."

"What do you mean, he's out?"

"It's innocent until proven guilty, Ella." Charlotte's voice had an edge that made Ella uncomfortable. They were supposed to be on the same side.

"All the evidence they have is incredibly circumstantial. I can't even believe they brought him up on charges."

Ella's vision blurred over as she stared out the windshield. Charlotte carried on until Ella couldn't take it anymore.

"Where did he get the money?" Ella asked, her voice beginning to crack. There was no answer. "Charlotte. Where did he get the *bail money?*"

Charlotte cleared her throat, but she didn't bother speaking. Ella knew where it had come from.

"What the fuck is wrong with you?"

"Excuse me?" Charlotte barked back.

"He murdered my husband. He murdered some innocent woman and buried her body on your old property. How could you ever defend him?"

Charlotte scoffed. "Ryan died of an overdose. The woman was shot with Ryan's gun. That's the whole story."

"That's the part of the story you want to pay attention to! She was buried on his land. Ryan was set up for a huge commission that they were going to hand over to Sam instead."

Tears streamed down Ella's face, but instead of sad, she just felt empty. She couldn't go on her entire life defending her husband and bringing all the blame down on his best friend. She would never win.

58

Tiana
May 6, 2022

She had been watching out the upstairs window when Clemens walked back up the steps to her front door. It must have taken him more time to get the warrant than he thought, since hours passed. She sat with the file folder she had curated for Nate in her lap. Half of it wasn't true. The rest of it was half-truths. Her father had always told her never to lie, but she'd never had to protect a teenage boy from murder charges before.

After she heard the firm knock of Clemens's hand against her door, she forced herself up and let out a breath she hadn't realized she was holding. Her lungs felt like they had shriveled once the air was out. Her chest ached.

She unlocked the door and pulled it open. Clemens stood with a smile on his face, his phone in his hand.

"Warrant is right here," he said, gesturing to the screen but not handing it to her.

"I'd like to take a look."

Clemens shrugged and handed her the phone. She zoomed and scrolled, verifying Nate's name on the warrant, as well as her own. With the phone back in Clemens's hand, she gripped the manilla folder between her hands so tightly the pages crinkled.

"Satisfied?" he asked. Tiana wanted to slap the smirk off his face with the folder.

I bet it felt amazing to hit Sam, she thought. Ella must have felt a wave of relief once she had done it. Except she knew she hadn't. Because instead, she was too focused on his accusation. An accusation that couldn't be far from the truth.

Tiana held out the folder with her right hand, using the left to hold onto the door. A strong breeze could have blown her over, and it was all she could do to stop her hand from shaking viciously.

"Any chance you want to hand over your laptop too?" He offered a false smile, and Tiana felt disgust swell inside her. She stepped back and swung the door shut, her frustration with him outweighing her fear.

The scales in her mind continually went back and forth with the idea that Nate had killed Kelly Carter. His story couldn't be entirely true. After all, he had been with Sophia when school let out. She had heard both their voices on the phone. Sophia was there, too, and just like Tiana was protecting Nate, she had a feeling he was protecting Sophia.

59

Sam
May 6, 2022

"This is bullshit!" Sam yelled, gesturing to his ankle monitor. "What the hell happened to innocent until proven guilty?"

Sam's public defender rolled his eyes. From the moment Sam first saw him, he thought he was a schmuck. He wore an oversized tweed suit jacket with beige slacks. He introduced himself as Bob McNeil. Sam's first thought when he saw the guy was that he was fucked.

Of course, his first phone call was to Charlotte. She must have heard the news, seen the mailbox on the news like everyone else had, and was not surprised when her phone rang with a collect call.

"Oh, Sam." The words fell out of her mouth like a sigh. He had heard that phrase filled with disappointment so many times before.

"Look, Charlotte, I know this looks bad, but it's all going to be okay. We can get me out of this." Sam felt his stomach twist when he said the words because he wasn't sure they were true. But he had to pretend he was confident about the entire ordeal; otherwise, he might look more guilty.

"Sam, I can't defend you. You know that."

Sam's stomach hit the floor. "No, I do *not* know that." He had to avoid hissing out the words.

"It–It just would ruin my reputation in the legal community. I cannot get up there and defend my husband, particularly when my other client is the wife of the man you allegedly murdered."

Sam had to admit it would look pretty bad. It was definitely better for Charlotte to distance herself as much as possible from her ex-husband. But that was also definitely worse for him.

"I get it. I do. You don't have to defend me. But maybe you can get somebody else to? Maybe they could do it pro bono as like a display of friendship? Or loyalty or something?" The phrase there's no loyalty among thieves came to mind, and Sam guessed it probably applied to lawyers too.

"No. I can't do that either." Sam could hear Charlotte struggling to get the words out. She felt bad, that much he could tell.

"Please, I just need a loan then. Give me the name of someone. I'll pay you back once I'm out of this." Sam hesitated. She knew he didn't have a damn thing to give her. And he doubted his job would take him back after this. It wasn't a good look, being accused of murdering a coworker, whether he was guilty or not. "I know money is tight, but I'll be able to pull it together. I swear."

"Sam, you will get a public defender. You are legally entitled to it. Some of them are good. Maybe you'll get lucky."

Now, Sam stared at Bob, and he knew Charlotte had jinxed it. He had certainly not gotten lucky, but the dipshit *had* gotten him out on bail. Except, with this GPS strapped to his ankle, he didn't feel very free.

"It was a compromise, Sam." Bob shook his head and stuffed his hands into his coat pockets.

"The only thing that is being compromised are my rights!" Sam's face was turning red now, and he could feel his blood surging through him. Sweat was leaking out of the pores on his forehead. He needed a hit of something to take the edge off. But with the GPS, there wasn't much he could do. And most dealers weren't willing to make a drop for someone on house arrest.

"Unfortunately, this is all we can do." Bob shrugged, and Sam resisted the urge to push him up against the wall and choke him out. Just imagining it made him feel better.

"Then get the fuck out of here."

"If that's what you want," Bob turned on his heels and headed for the apartment door. Sam shook his head and slunk down on his couch. He could feel a singular broken spring pushing into his back. If that wasn't a metaphor, he wasn't sure what was.

60

Ella
May 8, 2022

"Tiana, I need you to come over," Ella begged into the phone.

Tiana's voice had been groggy when she first answered the phone. It was four in the morning after all, and Ella had clearly woken her. Ella, on the other hand, was still wide awake.

"Okay. Can I ask why?"

They hadn't spoken much the past few days, with the exception of the phone call after she assaulted Sam at the jail. Ella hadn't particularly wanted to talk to her, or anybody, for that matter. At the end of the day, Sam had broken her trust, and she was scared. Scared that somebody else could do it too. Even if it wasn't him. There was enough evidence that still made him suspicious. And Ella wasn't taking many chances.

"I'm scared." Ella was hesitant to admit it. Since she had heard from Charlotte on Friday, she hadn't stopped thinking about Sam's release. How he was out on the streets. How he was mad at her. Mad at Nate. Mad at the world. If he was guilty, what was stopping him from striking again? If he wasn't guilty, what better motivation to go after the person he thought truly committed the crime?

Nate was in the room next to her. She was still holed up in the guest bedroom, unable to even walk into her bedroom without shaking.

"I'll be right there." Tiana hung up without asking any other questions. Ella hadn't told her Sam had been released, but maybe she knew. Maybe it was on the news. She had no idea. She'd been alternating between staring off into space all weekend and checking the locks on the windows and doors repetitively. She hadn't told the kids he was released, but they had to know something was very wrong.

Within ten minutes, Tiana's headlights appeared at the end of the street, and Ella felt relief wash over her. She wished she had Ryan's old gun. He wasn't a hunter, but he did have a handgun that he could use for defense if that time ever came. The conversation had not gone over well when he first bought it.

"Ella, honey, I just bought it so that I can keep our family safe."

Ella hadn't wanted to look at him. Her rage was mixed with pregnancy hormones.

"Nate is so little. What if he stumbles upon it? He is just learning how to walk now. And you want to put a weapon in his hands."

By some miracle, Ryan had avoided rolling his eyes. "Ella, I am not putting the gun in his hands. I bought a safe with a lock. You and I will know the combination. It will be perfectly safe."

"So, when some person breaks into our house and they have a gun since this is Texas, you just have a good old-fashioned shootout? That's the solution?" Ella shook her head, her arms crossed tightly over her chest.

"Having a gun is better than having nothing. And when the kids get older, we can show them how to properly use it. What the combination is. That way they can protect themselves too."

"Are you on drugs?" Ella's eyebrows were sky high.

Ryan came to her, placed both hands on her shoulders, and stared directly into her eyes.

"We have to consider that they won't always be kids. Someday, they are going to grow up and have to live in this messed-up world too. And I would rather them learn how to use a gun safely with us than to mess around at a friend's house and end up dead."

Ella shook her head at the memory. She couldn't help but think that somehow, it hadn't mattered in the end. The gun was meaningless. And now, when she might actually want it herself, it was in evidence lock-up somewhere.

She waited for Tiana to try the knob before she unlocked the door. Tiana had a key, but usually, Ella left it unlocked when she knew she was coming over. That was a thing of the past now.

"Hey," Tiana whispered softly as she glanced around the entryway, probably looking for the kids. They were both upstairs as far as Ella knew, hopefully sleeping peacefully since she couldn't.

"Come in." Ella ushered Tiana in so that she could close the door behind her. "Sit down." The sound of the deadbolt clicking into place brought her the smallest comfort. It wouldn't stop somebody from breaking the glass of the door, though. Or a window.

Tiana slid off her sneakers and trudged into the living room, shoving her hands into the pockets of her gray sweatpants.

Ella waited for them both to be settled on the sectional to start talking. She had thought about offering Tiana coffee, but she couldn't bring herself to. It seemed like it would take entirely too much energy. If she did that one thing, she thought it might even break her.

"Sam's out."

Tiana blinked, then shook her head. "No, he's not. What are you talking about? Did he like"—Tiana paused for a moment, blinking rapidly and shaking her head—"escape or something?"

"No. They *let* him out on bail. On Friday."

"No, they didn't," Tiana asserted. "They wouldn't do that."

"They *did*," Ella insisted. "And now I'm terrified for my life. For the kids. I haven't slept since."

"Guess I should have brought over Ollie." Tiana blinked several times. "Not sure how good of a guard dog he would actually be, but maybe he could at least scare Sam off?"

Ella shook her head. "He's met Ollie. Ollie wouldn't do a thing to anybody. Worst I've ever seen him do was eat flies."

Tiana absent-mindedly smiled. Ella wondered if Tiana felt as detached from reality as she did.

"None of this can possibly be happening, right? It's all just too ridiculous. It's just some terrible, awful dream that we're both going to wake up from." Ella bit her bottom lip, and Tiana didn't bother answering. They both knew the truth.

61

Tiana
May 8, 2022

They had both passed out on the living room sectional around six in the morning. Tiana woke up, her hair frizzy and her neck sore. Ella had remained asleep as Tiana stretched and struggled to make her way off the couch. She decided it was best to let her stay there, sleeping for as long as she could. In the daylight, things were safe.

Ryan's murder flashed in her memory, and she frowned. At least daylight used to seem safer.

On her way home, she decided to stop for some Starbucks as a treat. She tried to support local businesses, but there was nothing better than a Starbucks mocha to warm you up after a night of bad sleep.

It was a mistake though, going to get the coffee. She pulled onto the street before the turnoff and came to a dead stop. Cars were lined up, desperately trying to merge two lanes into one as police lights flashed in the right lane. The lights reflected off the glass windows of the building. Her eyes ran up and down the scene, straining to see around the other cars and parked vehicles.

A car honked behind her, and she jumped, realizing that the other cars had all begun to move forward, albeit slowly. Tiana threw her right hand up as an apology as she moved forward. There was no name on the front of the building—it was clearly an office building, probably of multiple businesses. But Tiana had a feeling she knew whose offices might be inside. And as she was just about to merge back into the right lane, her eye in the rearview mirror caught a face. Dave Clemens.

Tiana punched the buttons on the screen embedded in her car's console. A phone rang throughout her speaker before Ella's voice answered.

"Hello?"

Her voice was drenched with drowsiness. Tiana hadn't wanted to wake her, but now she felt like she needed to.

"Clemens is at Ryan's office building."

The image of Clemens on her front porch came flashing back to her.

"Why?"

Tiana huffed, frustrated by her cluelessness.

"They must be gathering more evidence. They aren't done with their investigation." Tiana's mind was focused on Nate, but she was surprised when Ella said the same.

"Nate?" Ella's voice came out so softly and with a sadness that Tiana hadn't heard from her. Goosebumps trailed up and down Tiana's arm, and she turned off the air conditioning in her car to try to shake the chills.

"Clemens came to my house. Friday." Tiana knew she should have said something sooner. "He was looking for my notes on my sessions with Nate."

Ella didn't respond, but Tiana could hear her breathing on the other line.

"Don't worry. There is nothing for them." Tiana remained vague so she didn't have to explain that Nate had told her something. That she just didn't write it down.

"I know," Ella answered, her voice hollow. Tiana had felt pretty good about herself for looking out for Nate even before she thought something might be amiss. But Ella's reaction made her question the decision. Clearly, her friend had just assumed that Tiana would have Nate's back. Instead of that making her feel more confident about their friendship, the realization made her feel so small that she wanted to curl up and die.

"It will be okay, Ella. Everything will be fine." Tiana's grip on the steering wheel tightened as she spoke.

"Will it?" Ella's words echoed in Tiana's head for the rest of the morning.

62

Sam
May 8, 2022

Sam had fallen asleep on his couch again, exhaustion hitting him like a freight train. Being in a jail cell didn't provide quality sleep, especially when you were sober in a jail cell. He didn't have any drugs now because he knew the police would be searching his house. The first two nights home, he had felt restless. He had wandered in a loop from his kitchen, around the second-hand couch in the living room, into the bedroom, and back again over a hundred times. Last night was the first time he got a good night's rest.

Sam had seen the news coverage of the cabin. He, too, watched as they discovered Kelly Carter's body. When he saw his own mailbox, he thought for a moment that he was having a horrible trip. He had figured that Kelly Carter was dead once he realized the kids were alive. But maybe she had just disappeared.

Ultimately though, she was found dead, and it certainly looked like he did it.

After the news broadcast, his instincts kicked in, even though his mind was slow on the uptake. He flew around the apartment in a flurry, grabbing anything he could flush, and making sure to hide the things he couldn't incredibly well. The police were at his door in no time, and it wasn't until he opened it that the idea finally hit him. Maybe somebody had set him up. Maybe somebody knew what he had done.

Now that he was out, all Sam could think about was Nate Thomas. Ella's words played on repeat in his mind. It probably took a lot for a mother to suspect their own child of murder. Ella wasn't going to give that up, though. What kind of a mother would she be if she did? And based on how hard he had slapped her, she was in serious denial of the situation.

As thoughts swirled around Sam's head, a noise at his apartment door broke his focus. It sounded like scratching, maybe a mouse in the walls, but more metallic. His eyes narrowed as he turned his head to focus on the sound. In his head, he imagined a battering ram on the other side—the police here to do yet another search. But a moment went by, and Sam realized it wasn't that at all. He heard the lock of his front door click, and a shiver went down his spine. Within a moment, he was on his feet, diving for the front door, hoping to hold it shut. But he was just too late.

A tall bald man stood in Sam's doorway but only for a second. He rushed into the apartment and shut the door behind him. Sam stood, inches from him now, uncertain of what was happening next. He didn't recognize him, and that made Sam's heart race more.

The man pulled a gun out of the back of his waistband. He pointed it in Sam's general direction, but he was holding it by his hip, not properly extending it. Sam did the calculations in his head to see if he could disarm the man since he was clearly unfamiliar with holding a gun, but thought better of it. He scanned the man's face, frantically looking for some clue of his identity. His eyes were bloodshot, and the skin around them was red, as though he had been crying. Sam put his hands in the air and took a step back, hoping to placate the man.

"Why did you do it?" the man barked, his voice unsteady. "Why did you hurt her?"

Sam blinked, stepping back. He opened his mouth to ask who but realized before the word came out. Kelly Carter.

"I didn't do it. I swear to God."

The man scoffed. "I really doubt a man like you worships any god."

If a gun wasn't pointed at him, Sam would have laughed. It was an accurate assessment.

"That's fair. But I am telling the truth."

Sam hadn't done it. He had planned on doing it, that was true. He had everything in his car to go in after Kelly Carter finished the job and take her down too. There was no way he was giving up any of the money he got from Ryan's death. He had planned out the scene in his head multiple times leading up to the murder. She would send a text, hopefully saying that the estimate was complete. He would sneak inside after her just as she was gathering her things. At the bottom of the staircase, he would poise himself and wait for her to round the corner. At the precisely right moment, he would put a needle into her neck and watch her drop to the ground. In his mind, this took seconds. In real life, he knew it would take longer. He had been prepared to struggle with her, if necessary, but he felt confident the element of surprise would be on his side. But then the plan had fallen to pieces when he saw the kids coming up the sidewalk.

He had been shocked when Charlotte had called to tell him that Ryan was dead. But only because it was just Ryan. The kids were safe and had been the ones to find him. He figured the plan had worked out for the best, in a way. He hadn't thought Nate would bury Kelly Carter on his property.

"Who did it then? Who!" The man's face was turning varying shades of red now, and the veins in his neck were visible.

Sam smiled and opened his mouth to speak.

63

Nate
May 9, 2022

"Nathaniel Thomas, please report to the front office. Nathaniel Thomas, to the front office."

"Shit," Nate murmured as he peeked out of the boy's bathroom. The halls were empty. He was supposed to be in English class, but he had told his teacher he was heading to the counselor because he was having *issues*. The teacher had pursed her lips and nodded, her eyes filled with concern. It was a lot easier to sneak around now that his dad had died. Teachers believed everything he said, or if they didn't, they felt bad enough not to say anything. But if they were calling for him, they already knew he wasn't in the counselor's office. That he had never even made it down there, despite leaving class 30 minutes ago.

Nate stuck his hands into his black hoodie and walked briskly down the hall, hoping not to draw too much attention but also trying to get there as fast as he could. He pulled open the door to the office to see Assistant Principal Meadows, standing behind the secretary. They both looked up as he walked in.

"Nate," Mr. Meadows said as he pushed open the door behind the front desk.

Nate hesitated before following him. He tried to count how many classes he had skipped since he had been back in school. After a minute, he decided it was easier to count how many he had actually attended. He barely reached double-digits.

"Hey," Nate mumbled as he followed Meadows down the hallway and into his office. He paused in the doorway, unsure of himself. Dave Clemens sat in one of the chairs in front of Meadows's desk.

"Hello, Nathan."

"It's Nate." His full name was Nathaniel, not Nathan. That alone probably would have been enough to set his mother off on Clemens.

"Grab a seat. I just had a few questions to ask." Clemens put on a big smile, and Nate felt sweat drip down his back.

"I think I'm good standing." Nate was still in the doorway. Meadows had settled down behind his desk, the chair squeaking under his large frame. He had been a football coach before joining the school's administration. Nate had always thought he was the kind of guy who spent his entire adult life chasing the high he got from playing high school football.

"Nate," Meadows cautioned.

Nate took one step forward into the room but still didn't move to the chair. He shoved his hands into the pockets of his jeans.

"That's fine." Clemens shrugged. "Anyway, I just wanted to go over a few inconsistencies in your—"

"Does my mom know you're here?" Nate asked, his eyes narrowing. He already knew the answer.

"In the state of Texas, I do not need a parent present to question a minor. Besides, you're 17." Clemens glanced at Meadows, who nodded in agreement. Nate's mouth turned sour with disgust.

"Then I want my lawyer." Nate held his chin up high. He was done playing games with these assholes. If they already thought he was guilty, there was no point in pretending anything otherwise.

"Nathan," Clemens chided. Nate had to hold himself back from punching him in the face. "You know it doesn't look good. We don't need to get anybody else involved in this. Do you really want to bother all the rest of these people? Don't you think your mom has been through enough?"

Nate took a step forward. "Do not talk about my mother."

Clemens lifted his hands up defensively. "Look, I already talked to Sophia, and she told me everything."

Nate swallowed hard. "I want my lawyer."

Clemens nodded and shrugged. "Have it your way."

* * *

The police hadn't said anything else to him after he stood his ground about wanting his lawyer, but it had been hard for Nate to do the same. Every fiber of his being was begging to ask them what Sophia had said. Sitting in the back of the patrol car, he stared down at his phone, debating if he should text her and ask. But then, could that be used as evidence? Would that make him seem more guilty?

A thought floated into Nate's head, and for whatever reason he couldn't shake it. What if Clemens had got it wrong? What if he meant Tiana had told him everything? Nate tried to shake out the bad thoughts. Tiana would never do that to him. He was fairly certain of it. Plus, she claimed they had confidential records.

Nate's eyes ran over the back of Clemens's head. It was balding at the peak, but he kept his hair short so most people wouldn't notice. It looked like he was a bit overdue for a trim. He probably hadn't gotten much sleep since this whole ordeal began. Probably a decent amount until they realized Kelly Carter was missing. Then it became more intense, since people actually seemed to care when a pretty white woman went missing.

Nate opened his mouth to speak, ready to berate Clemens for brushing off his dad's case. His brain tumbled from thought to thought, each idea like a singular rock in an avalanche. He had told himself that this moment might come. He might go to jail for the things he had done. But at least he had a reason.

64

Ella
May 9, 2022

"They want to take him down to the station now for questioning."

"What?" Ella sat amongst stacks of medical files on her living room floor. She had finally gotten focused on work when Charlotte had called. "Why?"

"I guess they have some evidence against him. I just spoke to Nate on the phone and told him to cooperate and go down there, and I would meet him. But he did say something to me," Charlotte paused, and Ella's heart stopped beating.

"What?"

"Clemens told him that Sophia told them the truth."

Ella was on her feet so fast that she felt faint. "What do you mean?" Her words spilled out venomously. She wasn't certain she even knew the truth—how could Sophia? And why would she do this to their family?

"I don't know any of the details. I'm getting in my car now to meet him at the station. I told him not to say a word."

"Of course not. I don't even think he should be doing this interview."

"Ella, we have to cooperate to a certain extent. And if they want to question him, we only have so many options. This is the easiest way, as long as I'm there."

Ella wanted to scream, but instead, she bit her bottom lip hard enough she could taste metal.

"Why did Sophia talk to them without you?" Ella knew that answer even though she had asked. If she wanted to turn in her brother for whatever role he had played in this, then why would she want a lawyer present? Sophia meticulously thought out every decision in her entire life. When she was a kid, she would spend 10 minutes deciding between two ice cream flavors. Ella's stomach twisted as she wondered if maybe Sophia was afraid of her brother, and that was why she had done it.

"Ella, are you listening?" Charlotte barked into the phone.

Ella blinked, slowly being pulled back into reality. "Yes, I am." She cleared her throat loudly.

"There is a chance that Sophia didn't say a word to them. I want to make that very clear. They can lie up and down, forward and back until they get a confession. I don't think we should be too worried about this."

"Sure, right. Of course." Ella thought somewhere in the back of her mind she had known that the police could lie.

"If you want to meet me at the station, you should. I don't think you should be in the room, but it might not be a bad idea to at least listen from outside."

Ella shook her head, her blonde hair swaying. "No. I have something else I need to get done."

"Suit yourself. I'll tell you everything when the interview is over."

Ella hung up, not liking the edge in Charlotte's voice. She was judging her for not showing up. But Ella knew she could only take so much more of this police business before she had a full-on mental break. Instead, she grabbed her car keys and headed out the door.

65

Sophia
May 9, 2022

"Let go of me!" Sophia cried out, desperately trying to get her wrist out of her mother's fierce grip.

They were in the school parking lot. Ella had pulled her out of the middle of class. When her name came on the overhead speaker, she felt like she was in a free fall. The kids all stared at her like they knew what it was about. Were the cops here to question her about her dad? Half the school thought her brother was the real killer. After all, what man would kill his best friend? The other half of the school thought her mom did it. She had managed to mostly stay out of the crossfire, but she hated the way her name was whispered under people's breaths in the hallway. And the way they all stared at her now, waiting for her to break.

"Miss Thomas," Mr. Fredericks called, and Sophia nodded.

"Should I take my stuff?" she had asked. He shrugged, and she decided she didn't want to come back even if she had time. With her loaded backpack hauled on, and her lunchbox in her hands, she made the trek to the front office, wringing the straps of the lunchbox with each step.

When she caught a glimpse of her mother through the glass of the front office, she felt relieved. At least if her mom was here, things couldn't be that bad. At least they weren't calling to tell her that her mom was in jail. Not that she thought that would happen.

But when she pulled open the office door and her mother turned to face her, Sophia felt her footholds go loose, and she was tumbling downward again. She hadn't seen such anger on her mother's face since her brother had dented her car's front bumper on a pole.

"Mom?" Sophia asked hesitantly. Her mother was dressed in loungewear topped with a long cardigan. Her arms were crossed tightly over her chest and she audibly exhaled when Sophia spoke.

"Come on," she spat, turning and heading toward the door.

Sophia tossed a glance at the receptionist behind the desk who just averted her eyes.

Thanks a lot, Sophia thought.

Ella had waited until they were out of view of the front office to grab Sophia's wrist.

"What are you doing?" Sophia whined, pain shooting up her arm.

"Don't you even pretend with me," she hissed, yanking her toward the car. Sophia's weight was thrown off, and she nearly toppled to the ground.

"You're hurting me!" Sophia yelled, and that seemed to penetrate through her mother's anger. Her fingers released Sophia's wrist, and Ella stared at her. "*What* is going on with you?"

Ella blinked, and for a moment, Sophia thought that this was the moment she had been waiting for. Her mother hadn't fallen to pieces, not really, since her dad had died. She got close the night they found out about the overdose, but she hadn't gone totally over the edge. Now with the way her eyes looked empty and how her expression was so neutral she looked dead, Sophia figured it had finally happened.

After a few seconds, Ella's eyes blinked rapidly and then opened wide. "Get in the car." Ella yanked her keys out of her purse and unlocked all the doors.

Sophia, knowing better than to argue, climbed into the passenger seat.

Once the doors were all shut, and Ella had turned on the car, Sophia decided to speak. "What's going on?"

"What did you say to Clemens?" her mother asked. Instead of angry, now she just sounded tired.

"Clemens? Detective Clemens?" Sophia asked after pausing a moment to place the name. Of course, his name was in the forefront of her mind, but she wasn't going to let her mother know that.

"Yes." Her mother exhaled deeply.

"Nothing."

"Nothing?" she asked, staring out the windshield.

"I didn't even see him. Why? What's going on?" Sophia felt panic rising inside her. Maybe Nate had decided to tell the truth. Maybe she was going down with the ship.

66

Nate
May 9, 2022

"I think it's about time you told me the truth," Clemens declared, pacing in the room. If he was doing that to make Nate feel anxious, it wasn't working. It just gave him something to watch while he ignored the question.

"I don't think that is a question, Dave," Charlotte leaned back in her chair, with her arms crossed over her chest. Nate wondered how she was able to put on such a good act. He knew she must be upset about Sam's arrest. But there was no sign of it on her face now.

Clemens stopped pacing and put his hands palm down on the metal table. Nate guessed that if Charlotte wasn't here, he would have done it a lot more forcefully.

"What happened when you got home?"

"Sophia and I got home late from a review session and we went upstairs. We found his body." Nate was very careful to use the word 'we.'

"That's not what you told Ms. Hill."

Nate felt shivers climb up and down his body. "What?" His mouth was slightly ajar. There was a faint ringing in his ears.

"Ms. Hill told us everything. She had to. It was a court order. She had to hand over all the files," Clemens continued.

Nate stared on in shock, unable to pull himself together. He felt Charlotte touch his arm.

"Nate, don't say anything."

Nate turned to look at Charlotte, but he didn't really see her.

"Come on, Nate. Just confess. Tell me what happened. It's the only way." Clemens stared down at him, and Nate met his gaze. He felt like the blood was disappearing from his body. Somewhere, far away, he could hear Charlotte protesting as he opened his mouth.

Instead of answering Clemens, he vomited all over the metal table.

67

Ella
May 9, 2022

"Mom, what is going on?" Sophia begged from the passenger seat. Ella had turned the SUV on and had planned on going down to the police station to stop Nate from saying anything. But her brain was on autopilot, so instead, she was pulling into their driveway before she knew it.

"Is Nate talking to Clemens? Right now?"

Ella could hear the building desperation in her daughter's voice. All her fears were true then. Nate had done it. Or some of it. Maybe all.

"Yes," she choked out as she pulled into the driveway.

"Well, we need to go see him."

"Charlotte is there." Ella shifted the car into park and looked at her daughter critically. "What do you need to tell him?"

Sophia looked away from her mother and let out a deep breath. "I just—" For just a moment, she got too choked up to speak. "I just want him to know that I didn't say anything. That I would never do anything to hurt him. And if he has anything he needs to tell the police"—she paused again, holding back a sob—"then he should tell them the truth."

A sob now fell from Ella's face like it caved in on itself. Sophia sat unmoving for a moment before reaching out and touching her mother's arm.

"No," Ella gasped between breaths. Everything disappeared for a moment. She couldn't feel Sophia's hand touching the goosebumps on her arm. She was no longer sitting in the SUV but drowning in a lake while spectators watched. And right there, in the center of them all, was Nate. Watching her die.

"Let's get inside, Mom. People will notice," Sophia whispered urgently.

Ella bit her bottom lip and pulled in a sharp breath. Sophia was right. Even if Ella had to be burdened with the truth, that didn't mean everyone else had to know. She wasn't sure yet if that was what she wanted. Even if her son had killed the love of her life, he was still her son. Or was he? How much could you overlook when it was your own child? Ella wasn't sure, but she knew she wasn't ready to decide yet. She gripped the door handle for a long moment before the tears dried up.

"Let's go," she whispered to Sophia, her stomach lurking in her throat.

The pair climbed out of the car and hurried to the house.

"Give me the keys," Sophia ordered, holding out her hand. The tears were gone from her face now. Ella always knew Sophia was the one to rise to action when others were in crisis. Even if she was distraught, she was able to lock it away until she helped someone else. It made her a lot like Tiana. At the same time she found Nate breaking her heart, she could feel Sophia holding the pieces together.

Ella shook her head. "I left it open. I was in a hurry." She reached out a shaky hand and pushed the door open. The pair flurried into the house, and Ella slammed the door shut once Sophia cleared the frame. She let out a very slow breath, trying to regain control.

"Hey ladies," a voice called out from the foyer, and Ella's eyes flicked up instantly.

She found herself staring down the barrel of a gun, a ray of sunlight sparkling on the barrel. Ella swallowed hard and looked at Sophia. Her hands were already in the air. And so Ella did the same.

68

Sophia
May 9, 2022

Sophia hadn't even turned to look at her mother once her eyes had locked onto the man. The smirk painted across his face was so extreme that he appeared like a monster. He was chewing on a piece of gum, his lips smacking with satisfaction as he watched their responses. Only one hand held the gun. Sophia recognized it as a 9-millimeter and swallowed hard. If it had been a revolver, maybe they could've had a chance to rush him. But there was enough distance between them and him that he would surely have time to fire at them. There were enough bullets that he could afford to miss a few times.

She wondered if her mother had come to the same conclusion but decided she didn't know enough to do the calculations. The odds were not in their favor. Even if Sophia spun around and rushed out the door, by the time she got it open, he could get off at least two, maybe three shots. There was no other option but to give up.

Her father had taught her how to shoot when she was 13. In the car on the way to the woods, he had a long talk with her, telling her about how he wanted her to be the safest possible person she could be. Sophia had agreed with him. She did need to learn to protect herself, especially in the world they lived in. Apparently, her mother hadn't received the same training.

"Aren't you two a lovely surprise," he mocked, his eyes narrowing in on them.

Sophia could feel the panic radiating off her mother. She had certainly been wrong earlier. *This* would be the thing to break her.

"If you are looking for money, we don't have any," Ella sputtered. Sophia could see her hands shaking out of the corner of her eye.

The man threw back his head and laughed. He was mostly bald, but Sophia could make out a few patches that were missed when he last shaved his head. His beard was sparse, and she saw a black hole in his mouth where a tooth was missing.

"Oh no, no, no, I'm not interested in money." He swaggered a bit closer to the pair but still kept his distance.

He was smart enough to do at least that, Sophia thought.

Ella let out half a whimper as he approached. She took a partial step in front of Sophia, trying to block his access to her. Sophia grimaced as she watched her mother struggle to be brave. She wished she wouldn't bother.

"Who are you?"

"Name's Tony. Nice to meet you," he chirped, the nauseating smirk back on his face.

"Why are you here?" Ella's words tumbled out, growing more frantic with each syllable.

"Now isn't that a good question." Tony lowered the gun but kept it at the ready. "Where's Nate?"

Sophia felt the urge to push her mother out of the way, to bum-rush the man. It wouldn't work though. And she was not interested in getting shot today.

"He's not here," Sophia spoke up when her mother hesitated a moment too long.

"No shit," he spat, raising the gun again. "Get in the living room. Now!"

Sophia watched his face become unhinged as his eyes darkened and his eyebrows grew together.

Sophia lowered one of her raised hands onto her mother's shoulder.

"Come on," she whispered, trying to guide her. Eventually, Ella's legs moved. They had to walk past him to get into the living room, so he backed up into the kitchen, the gun still raised. Ella trudged forward, but Sophia glanced back at the door. She could get away, maybe, if she sprinted. He might shoot her mother, but what were the chances the both of them didn't end up dead anyway? The odds didn't look good.

"Don't you even think about it," he snapped, taking a step closer to her, the gun pointed directly at her head now. Sophia's eyes widened. The front door wasn't an option. So, Sophia did what she did best—she complied.

69

Nate
May 9, 2022

"I'm—" Nate was about to apologize for the vomit he had gotten on Clemens's hand, but stopped himself. He clutched his stomach. It was contracting, and he wondered if this was what a period felt like.

Charlotte watched in horror, unsure what to do. She didn't have a maternal bone in her body.

Nate bent over now, his head between his knees, as he began dry heaving, bile etching away at his throat and dripping to the floor.

An exasperated Clemens shook the vomit off his hand and turned to leave the room. Out of the corner of Nate's eye, he could see Clemens's body heave as though he was going to be sick too.

Charlotte's chair scraped against the floor as she pushed it back before the vomit had time to spread and spill onto her lap.

"This is a first." She stared at the scene, her hands resting on her hips, unsure what to do. After a moment, her eyes narrowed. "Nate, did you take something?"

Nate heaved twice more before he wiped his mouth with the back of his hand and sat up. He looked at Charlotte and shook his head. The room appeared to be spinning even when he stopped moving his head. "No."

"Are you lying?" She leaned forward, staring at his eyes to check his pupils.

"No," he repeated, more forcefully this time. His body was racked by another heave, but nothing was left. Charlotte took a step back just in case.

Clemens came back into the room, a custodian in the doorway. "I think we should postpone the rest."

His face looked clammy, and if Nate hadn't felt so disgusted, he would have been pleased with himself for making Clemens feel ill. Instead, he just felt miserable.

He had no explanation for why he was so sick, other than from what Clemens had told him. They were closing in on the truth, and it was only a matter of time before he faced the consequences. There were only two viable options in his head: keep his mouth shut and make more of a mess or confess with a lie. Telling the truth wasn't an option.

70

Ella
May 9, 2022

Ella and Sophia were stationed side by side on the couch. Tony paced the length of the room, and Ella watched as his finger tightened and then relaxed on the trigger of the gun. She squirmed each time he paused to stare at them. Time felt like it was at a standstill, and Ella continuously looked at the large wooden clock above the fireplace mantel. For once, she hoped Nate got arrested. Then he wouldn't come home to this. But at the same time, if Nate never came back home, what would happen to her and Sophia?

Ella's gaze shifted over to her daughter, who appeared to be squirming uncomfortably. Ella's eyebrows knitted together, and she leaned forward to get a better look at her daughter's face.

Tony's attention snapped back to them. "What?"

His behavior had grown more erratic since he arrived. She wondered if maybe he was a drug user and that was what possessed him to do something like this.

"I have to go to the bathroom," Sophia whispered, nervousness painted on her face. Ella thought that her poor daughter was so scared that she was regressing back into her childhood self. All of the sudden, she looked a lot younger than she was.

"No." Tony shook his head like it was a no brainer. "You can piss yourself."

Sophia bit her bottom lip for a moment. Ella reached out and squeezed her daughter's hand, hoping to reassure her.

"It's not that—" Sophia shifted again. "I got my period."

Tony's face instantly grew red. Ella could see the mental debate going on in his head. Finally, he spoke.

"Come here," he spat. Sophia started to get up, but he shook his head and pointed the gun at Ella. "You."

Ella slowly rose, her legs shaking. If she ever got out of this alive, she knew she would see the barrel of his gun pointing at her every time she closed her eyes.

"Come on," he spat, gesturing for her to hurry up with the gun. She forced one foot after the other. Finally, she stood before him. He reached out with his right arm, still holding the gun, and pulled her to him. His arm was looped around her neck, the barrel of the gun kissing her temple. Ella almost tried to slip away, but then she remembered his finger tightening and relaxing on the trigger and held herself still. He licked his lips, and she could feel the sweat from his arm against the back of her neck. "Good girl."

Ella saw her daughter cringe at his words, and she felt a level of humiliation she had never experienced.

"Give me your phone," he ordered, holding out his free hand. Sophia reluctantly stood and scooped the phone out of her back pocket. His hands closed around it and he turned slightly before throwing the phone directly at the fireplace. Both women jumped and Ella let out a squeal as his arm tightened around her in response.

"Go. We will be right here." He used the gun to brush some hair away from Ella's eyes.

"I have to go upstairs. That's where all my stuff is."

"You have two minutes."

Sophia nodded quickly, then turned and ran to the foyer and up the stairs.

"She doesn't have anything to do with this," Ella pleaded once she heard Sophia's feet hit the second floor.

Tony readjusted his grip on her, using his left arm to hold her steady now.

"So what? You want me to let her go so she can run off and get help? Tell people I'm holding you hostage?" Darkness fell over his eyes and his mouth twitched. Disgust transformed his face into something horrifying, and Ella panicked. It had been the wrong thing to say. "You might think I'm a fucking idiot, but I'm not dumb!"

Spit flew from his mouth and landed on Ella's cheek. She forced her eyes and mouth shut.

Ella didn't speak again, and after a few seconds, Tony called out, "Thirty seconds!"

The toilet flushed upstairs, and Ella hoped her daughter would just run. She didn't want her to come back down to this living room to die. Or watch her mother and brother die. But within what felt like two seconds, she heard Sophia rushing back down the stairs and into the living room. She cursed inside her head.

"Sit back down," he ordered, the gun briefly pointing at Sophia instead. She lifted her hands up and sidestepped over to the sectional. Ella watched her daughter settle into her seat. He didn't let her go.

"She's back," Ella whispered. "Can I sit back down?"

"No," he growled. "Not until your son gets home. And if that's not soon, we're gonna play a very special game called bang."

Ella's eyes fell on her daughter, and finally, for the first time, she totally fell apart.

71

Nate
May 9, 2022

"Let's go." Charlotte was already at the door of the interrogation room, ready to slip past Clemens.

Nate forced himself up, wiping his hands on his pants. There wasn't much on them, but enough that he could still smell vomit after he followed Charlotte out to the parking lot. She unlocked her car and looked him up and down.

"Shit," she murmured. "Get in." She rolled her eyes and settled in behind the wheel. Charlotte rolled down all the windows in the car, and it helped bring the smell of vomit down to a faint, lingering odor.

"Do you still feel sick?" she asked when he didn't speak inside the car. They were on the main drag now, and wind whipped through the windows. Charlotte struggled to keep her hair out of her face.

"No," he murmured. He did, but not in the way he had earlier. There wasn't an urgency anymore. Instead, he just felt like his fate was slowly circling the drain.

"Did you *actually* feel sick in there?"

Nate paused to contemplate this. He had felt incredibly nauseous, but it was a visceral reaction to what was happening, not food poisoning or the flu.

"Yes," he decided.

Charlotte nodded and accelerated a bit. Nate figured she couldn't wait to get him out of the car.

The silence returned, but Nate didn't mind. He needed time to think about what his next step was. What was he going to tell Sophia? What about his mom? And Tiana. Nate let out a slow sigh. He didn't blame her for what she had done. He was just some kid, really.

"Nate, we need to talk about all this." Charlotte was pulling off Main Street and heading toward his house.

"What's there to talk about?" he asked nonchalantly. He'd rather sit in silence right now.

"You need to take some time and really think about what you want to do here. Clemens has a look in his eyes. He's out for blood, and he's convinced you're the one he should go after." Charlotte paused, and Nate wondered if she was thinking about Sam right now. He wanted to ask if she thought he did it, but that didn't matter. Not really.

"So, you need to act now before your options are too limited. If it were me, I would take a plea deal. I know it's not necessarily the best outcome, but Nate—" She was staring over at him with such intensity that Nate worried she would crash into one of the parked cars in his neighborhood. She turned her eyes away as they approached a stop sign. "You need to consider what they might have on you. I don't know what they are telling the truth about and what they are lying about. But I have a feeling that you might."

Nate felt his chest get tight, and he swallowed hard. The back of his throat burned a little. He kept his mouth shut.

"You don't have to decide now. And you don't have to tell me what you may have done. I'm your lawyer. I will defend you as long as you want. But at the end of the day—" She shrugged, and Nate decided she was on Sam's side. She believed that Nate had truly killed two people—one being his own father, nonetheless—in cold blood. He didn't bother defending himself. He knew that it wasn't true.

72

Ella
May 9, 2022

A car door slammed, and Ella yelped. Sophia stared at her mother, unable to look away. Ella wished she would.

Tony didn't have to speak. Ella heard his breathing speed up, and she wanted to yell out for help. But there was nobody. It was one of those surreal experiences every adult has where you felt like the situation you were in was out of control, so you do what you always did as a child: You try to find an adult to help. Except you are the adult now. And Ella didn't know what to do either.

"Don't say a fucking word," he spat as he listened for the front door. The gun was still poised at Ella's temple, and she stared at her daughter. She figured there was an 80 percent chance the man blew out her brains and Nate's too. Sophia might make it out alive if she ran fast enough.

Ella listened as Nate fiddled with his key in the front door. She wished that just this once he had forgotten it. Her stomach was squeezing up into her throat, and she couldn't pull in the air she needed. Dots speckled her vision, and she thought for a moment that she might pass out. Tony's arm had tightened around her throat in his excitement, and she wrapped a hand around his arm, trying to gently give herself more room. It didn't matter, though, because in just a moment, the door swung open, and he released her.

Ella tumbled to the ground, her legs nearly asleep from him holding her for so long. She gasped for breath and closed her eyes. She didn't really want to see what happened next.

Nate's footsteps traveled down the foyer. There was another set of footsteps too. Heels. Ella didn't dare open her eyes, but she envisioned Charlotte coming down the hallway. But what if it was Tiana?

Thoughts flickered inside her mind. What if one of them was in on this? What if one of them helped Tony find Nate? After Sam, nothing was impossible. Or was it? If Nate really had done this, like Sophia had suggested in the car, then maybe Sam hadn't done anything wrong. Maybe he was just caught in the crossfire. Maybe she had focused her attention and anger and rage on the wrong person all along.

Her brain didn't want to go there, but the intrusive thought came all the same. Would it be so bad if Nate was killed? If he was the one who caused this entire mess, was that the worst-case scenario?

Charlotte squealed and her purse hit the ground with a thunk and Ella's eyes snapped back open. Tony had the gun poised at Nate, who stopped, dumbfounded. His arms remained by his sides as his eyebrows knit together. He wasn't processing what was happening.

"You piece of shit," Tony spat. Ella could hear tears in his voice now. She wondered if he loved Kelly Carter.

"What?" Nate asked. He sounded like a kid again, confused by the world. He had always been so curious when he was little, asking a million questions until Ella just about lost her mind. It only made sense it would happen again now.

A gunshot rang out, followed quickly by a second, and Ella's eyes snapped shut so hard it hurt.

73

Sophia
April 25, 2022

Sophia's hand was shaking now. She couldn't believe the scene before her eyes. In fact, she had done it all without thinking.

She had walked up the stairs and had planned on heading into her bedroom. But then she heard a sound coming from her parents' bedroom. Coughing. Nobody should be home. She would have *never* agreed to skip school and come home if she had thought for a minute one of her parents was here. She paused, listening more intently now.

Slowly, she made her way toward the noises, trying to clarify what they were. It was a rustling, like someone digging through a cabinet or closet, searching for something. Maybe it was simply her father, home, trying to find something for work. Her suspicions were proved partially correct when she reached the doorway and saw her father on his bed. But his black leather shoes were still on his feet. He was on his back, unmoving. Sophia blinked, confusion inching onto her face.

She took a step forward into the room. Her father wasn't the one making noise. There was someone in their parents' walk-in closet. It was a small closet, but the way it ran alongside their bedroom with only a small door prevented her from seeing inside. Her mother's SUV hadn't been in the driveway, and only her father could fit his car in the garage. There was no way it was her mother.

She edged toward her father, careful not to make a sound. As she got closer, she turned her eyes toward him, looking him over. She reached out a hesitant hand and touched his neck. She could feel a faint pulse, or at least she thought she could. She hadn't really ever felt somebody who didn't have a pulse before.

"Dad," she whispered, her voice urgent. She shook his body slightly, but he had no reaction. He lay on the bed, his eyes shut softly, his arms flayed out on his sides.

She heard a floorboard creak in the closet, and her body flew into action. Her hand pulled open the top drawer of her father's nightstand. He had kept his handgun in a safe when they were kids, but now that they were older—now that they knew what they could do with a gun—it simply sat in the drawer, unloaded. The drawer squeaked as she pulled it open so she kept her eyes locked on the closet entryway as she loaded a magazine into the gun. It made a satisfying click as she did so, but she wasn't worried about noise anymore. She had the upper hand. Her hand was trained on the closet, waiting to fire.

Her ears hyper focused on the noises of the house. Sophia heard Nate downstairs opening the fridge. The HVAC system was off. It was warm enough during the day that they didn't need heat, but not quite time for air conditioning. Nate was kicking his shoes off downstairs, and she could hear him gradually turn the TV up. It was only a matter of time before whoever was on the other side rounded the corner. Sophia felt her heart beat steadily, strongly. Her father had trained her for this exact moment, after all.

74

Nate
April 25, 2022

Nate was stuffing sour-cream-and-onion chips into his mouth when the first gunshot rang out. He dropped the bag, his eyes narrowing. It had been loud, loud enough that it sounded like it was inside the house. He told himself that wasn't possible, but the way the noise reverberated inside his head told him otherwise.

He jumped to his feet, the bag of chips tumbling to the ground.

"Sophia!" he called as he rounded the corner into the foyer, heading for the stairs. "Sophia!" This time, it was a frantic scream.

His hand grabbed the banister, and he used it to help swing him around the corner and onto the stairs. He took them two at a time, his vision blurring. Had his sister been upset enough that she would kill herself? The thought nagged on his brain, weighing him down. He first checked her room, but it was untouched.

"Fuck," he whispered, closing the door and turning around to see his parents' open bedroom door. As far as he knew, the only gun in the house was kept next to his dad's side of the bed. If she was going to do it, it would be in there.

"In here," Sophia called, her voice neutral.

Nate's eyes closed in relief. He took a step forward until he could see inside the bedroom. The relief disappeared instantly.

"Sophia," he whispered, staring at the scene. His father lay on the bed, unmoving, but untouched by the gun. Near the entryway to the closet lay a woman he didn't recognize. There was a gaping wound in her chest, and there was so much blood that Nate didn't know what to think. It looked so much worse than it did in the movies. His stomach lurched as he stood in the doorway, physically unable to step farther inside.

"She was an intruder," Sophia stated, blinking rapidly.

"Dad?" Nate saw the way he was lying. Something about it didn't strike him as natural.

"I think she killed him." Sophia stepped back, the gun still in her hands. Nate felt the urge to take it from her, but he knew better.

"Did you check for a pulse?" Nate asked.

"Of course, I checked!" Sophia snapped, her eyes wild. Nate put his hands up as if she was actually pointing the gun at him. "There was nothing. He's dead."

Nate's head swirled, and he ran his hand through his hair.

"We have to call the police. Maybe they can still save him. Maybe it hasn't been too long that—"

Sophia fired the gun again, this time into her father's stomach.

Nate jumped, scrambling backwards against the bedroom wall as he watched his father's body lie limp against the bed. He watched redness spread across the floral bedspread, and for a minute, he thought he might black out.

"What are you doing?" he asked, sadness blooming in his voice. Tears welled up in his eyes and tumbled down his face one after another.

Sophia had blood splatter on her hands now, and one stray speck on her face.

"Nate, he was already gone."

"But why would you do that to him!" he begged.

Sophia picked up a tissue from the box on her parents' dresser and wiped the gun's grip and trigger. She held the gun by the tissue before dropping it on the bed near her father's hand. After stepping away, she stuffed the tissue into her pocket.

"Nate, he was already dead."

Nate shook his head so violently it hurt. "You don't know that." He was now on the ground outside the bedroom, lying in a heap. "You didn't need to hurt him more."

Sophia frowned, but she didn't step forward to comfort him. "I did, though. Nate—" Sophia let out a slow breath. Nate was shaking his head still, his eyes shut so tightly he looked like a newborn baby crying. "Listen to me!"

Nate kept crying but stopped shaking his head. He stared up at his younger sister with a feeling of absolute dread.

"Are you listening?" she asked, her face stern. Nate nodded. "Good. If people found out that I killed someone, even if it is in self-defense, it would ruin me. Ruin my chances for a good college. Ruin everything. Do you understand?"

Nate felt like his chest was going to explode. "Yes," he squeezed out, his lungs feeling heavy.

"Will you help me?" she asked. Nate knew it wasn't a question though. He had no other choice.

Outside, the rain began to pour.

75

Sophia
April 25, 2022

"Nate," Sophia whispered softly. He was driving their father's car down the highway with her in the passenger seat. The rain had started to slow down as they got farther from their home. Luckily, their father's car had been parked in the garage.

Nate kept his eyes locked on the road. He was no doubt thinking about the body in the trunk. It had been her idea to take the woman to Sam's cabin, an idea that had come to her easily. It was remote. It had no connection to this whole ordeal. It was perfect.

Nate didn't answer, and Sophia was growing increasingly nervous. She fiddled with a loose string on her shirt.

Moving the body had been more difficult than she had anticipated. The woman looked a lot lighter than she actually was. Given that she was dead weight, it had been a struggle to even drag her across the floor in the tarp they had grabbed from the garage. Nate spent most of that time crying. Sophia snapped at him, warning him not to get any DNA on the scene, but she figured it might already be too late. If they found the body, they would be screwed anyway.

"It's all going to work out," she lied, the words slipping easily off her tongue. "There's nothing to worry about. Aunt T isn't even suspicious." Tiana had called just as they finished loading the body into the trunk. They had argued over whether they should answer when she called Nate's phone, but ultimately, he made the choice.

Nate glanced at her. Sophia found herself staring at the bloodshot veins in his eyes, and she knew she had messed up. To save her future, she had destroyed her brother's life. He wouldn't recover from this. He wasn't strong like she was.

Sophia kept her mouth shut the rest of the drive. Nate was careful about the speed limit, only ever going a few over to keep up with traffic. He pulled off and headed down the winding road to the cabin, still not speaking. No more tears came, and Sophia was grateful because she didn't think she could handle them if they did.

As they pulled up the road, Sophia bounced her legs, eager to get to work.

"Where should I park?"

"Just stay on the driveway; we don't want to leave any tire tracks."

Nate paused, looking over at Sophia. "Sam has the same car as Dad."

Sophia blinked. She hadn't thought about that. "He does."

"The tire tracks wouldn't matter," Nate explained, but Sophia's brain had already put the connection together. It was in that moment she fully decided where to put the blame.

76

Nate
April 25, 2022

Sweat dripped down his back as he lifted dirt off the pile and down into the grave.

"It's definitely too shallow," he argued, pausing a moment to stretch out his back.

"I know that. It's too late now. We need to get back." Sophia was like a machine, taking shovel after shovel of the dirt, not pausing. The ground was wet, which made their job easier but coincidentally, the dirt much heavier. Her breath was rapid, and Nate felt scared. He'd never seen Sophia like this, not once in their entire lives. He had seen the look of determination in her eyes but never in this way. There was fire behind it—anger even.

"Sophia, they are going to find her," Nate emphasized as he gestured down at the tarp in the ground. It was clear but blurred most of the woman's face, and Nate felt sick each time he stared at the makeshift grave a little too long.

"*I know*," Sophia panted, exasperated. "That is the *entire* point, Nate."

Nate blinked, stepping away from the hole.

"Wait what are you talking about? Why would you want them to find her?"

Sophia rolled her eyes. "Keep shoveling."

"No, I need to know what you mean," Nate insisted, taking another step back and dropping the shovel. It landed in the large pile of dirt they had unearthed.

"We need a backup plan. So I made one."

Nate's eyebrows knitted together. "What's this plan?"

Sophia glanced at the cabin barely visible through the woods.

Nate followed her eyes, landing on Sam's cabin. He blinked, his mind not wanting to believe what he thought she was suggesting.

"*Him?*" Nate asked, an air of desperation in his voice.

Sophia sighed, looked back down at the hole, and continued to pile in the dirt.

"Sophia, no, we cannot do that!" He reached out, trying to grab the shovel out of Sophia's hands. She pulled it away and raised it over her head. Nate put his hands in the air, eyes locked on his sister.

"We have to," she grunted, waiting for him to make a move.

Tears were starting to fall again, and Nate shook his head. It was all too much. He couldn't handle all this.

"I'm done."

"No, you're not," Sophia barked, lifting the shovel higher.

Nate wondered for a second if he should call her bluff. Worst-case scenario, she took him out, and he could wash his hands of this giant mess. Best case, she caved and they figured out a different solution. There were times in his life when he wouldn't have minded dying, even in the brutal way she was threatening. But now was not one of those times. A dead husband was enough. His mom didn't need a dead child too. He picked his shovel out of the dirt, and with his head down, got to work, tears still streaming down his face.

77

Sophia
May 9, 2022

Sophia's hand was steady, but the rest of her body felt like it was vibrating. She stared down the barrel of the gun she held, watching as Tony crumbled to the ground. It took her a moment to process that she needed to make sure the man was dead. But from the way he folded to the ground, she was pretty sure.

She put the gun into the waistband at the back of her jeans as she stood up. Charlotte was on the ground, checking Nate's pulse. Sophia walked over and stared at the pool of blood around Tony's head and felt satisfied that he was gone.

"Call 9-1-1," Sophia ordered, and she passed out of the living room and into the kitchen. She grabbed several tea towels from a drawer and returned, pushing them against Nate's wound. Apparently, Tony was a crappy shot, since he hit Nate's leg. It looked like the bullet went through his calf without hitting any major arteries. She hadn't decided how she felt about the outcome of events yet. Tony was dead, but she had also somewhat counted on Nate dying too. In a way, this complicated things.

Charlotte was rummaging through her purse now, urgently searching for the cell phone that was normally glued to her hand. Eventually, it was out, and she was talking to a dispatcher, her voice frantic.

Sophia tuned out her words as she stared down at Nate. His eyes were squeezed shut, as if he was pretending it wasn't happening. Her hands gripped his leg tightly, pushing the white-and-blue tea towels into the wound.

Ella had finally come around after she'd collapsed onto the floor. She let out a scream when she saw the blood pooling around Tony's body, and then scrambled across the floor on all fours, trying to make her way to Nate. Sophia nearly smiled when she imagined her mother as a soldier. She wouldn't make it through basic training, that was for sure.

"Where did that come from?" Ella demanded, staring at the gun Sophia had tucked in her waistband.

"Dad gave it to me for my sweet sixteen."

Sophia hadn't thought it was possible for her mother to look more shocked than she had already.

"You've had it this whole time?"

"I got it when I went upstairs. My period's not due for another week." She shrugged like it was no big deal. The gun had been hidden in a loose piece of floorboard in her bedroom. She was lucky the cops hadn't found it.

Ella shook her head. Her mother had never liked guns, which was why her dad hadn't told her about it. It had been their little secret.

Nate let out a low groan. Sophia's eyes snapped back to him.

"Am I dying?" Nate finally asked.

"Not this time," she replied, a small smile reaching her lips.

"It feels like I am," he groaned.

Sophia let out a laugh, but the way it burst out of her body felt inappropriate. Nate smiled reflexively, but it didn't last long.

78

Tiana
May 9, 2022

"How are you feeling?" Tiana asked, rising from her seat next to the hospital bed as Nate rustled.

Nate let out a hefty groan, and worry pushed her eyebrows together. She touched his forearm, searching his face for a sign of what he needed.

"I'm fine," he grunted, forcing his eyes open. "It's just really bright in here."

Tiana let out a sigh of relief that felt like she was finally casting off all her worries. Ella had called from the hospital immediately after everything happened. Her hands were shaking as she listened to her speak.

"Things have been less than ideal," Ella had started. Tiana figured that was the understatement of the century. "But I know Nate cares about you a lot. You are a role model to him."

Tiana hadn't been sure how true that was, but it still meant a lot to hear it.

"He's in the hospital. He was shot. He is okay, recovering, actually. He's asleep right now, but I think he would be really happy to see you when he wakes up."

Tiana had nearly dropped the phone when Ella spoke.

"Who?" Tiana had stuttered, the ability to form sentences lost for now.

"Long story. But—" Ella had let out a slow breath, and Tiana rested her right hand on her heart, willing it to slow down. "I think everything is going to work itself out. Maybe."

The questions Tiana wanted to ask piled up, but they were all just building blocks to her foundational question. "Is he going to take the fall?"

Ella hadn't seemed to be taken aback by the question. There was no gasp or accusation. Just a quick reply. "No."

That was when Tiana had started crying. Tears of relief, but so many other complex emotions. At the end of the day, she felt traumatized.

Now, hearing Nate complain about the amount of light in the room made those tears come back. He had come back to her. Tiana had always joked that he was her adopted son since he always tagged along after her like a duckling. She was worried he would be lost forever. But here he was, on the other side, alive. And nothing could darken that.

79

Nate
May 9, 2022

"Thanks," Nate managed as Tiana rushed to shut the blinds and turn off the overhead lights in the room. It was still like daylight because of the thin curtains, but enough that his head was no longer pounding.

"How's that?" she asked, returning to his side, her fingers resting on the bed, almost touching his arm. He nodded, which hurt a little, but managed to move his hand to hers. Her slender fingers curled around his, and he wondered if she was about to sob since it sounded like a cry was caught in her throat. She didn't though. She just plastered on this surreal smile that reminded Nate of being a kid. Of blowing out candles on birthday cakes. Of giving her hugs when she showed up at the house. She was his rock. His ship in the storm.

"Better."

"Good." Her words escaped like a joyful laugh.

"Aunt T." There were a thousand things he wanted to say. He knew now, staring at her face, that she would never have told Clemens any details from the sessions. He was a fool to think otherwise. He wanted to tell her that he was sorry for burdening her with the half-truth he had told. He hadn't wanted to tell her anything about that day. But eventually, it had all grown too big inside him, and if he didn't talk to someone, it would've started oozing out uncontrollably.

Tiana immediately shook her head at him. "You don't have to say anything. You don't ever have to explain yourself to me."

The corners of Nate's mouth upturned into a tiny smile. He squeezed her hand and looked toward the doorway, watching a nurse walk past.

"It sounds like you might even get to go home tomorrow. You're healing fast."

"No rest for the wicked," he joked, which brought a smile to her face.

Nate's brain flashed back to the last time he had pulled out that phrase. He thought of his sister with a gun in her hand. Twice.

"Nate, are you okay? What's the matter?" Tiana, of course, had immediately caught the shift in his face. She was good at her job.

"Sophia."

"She's fine. In fact, the news is talking her up like a hero. It's really wild." Tiana shrugged. "She said she thinks she'll be a shoe-in for an Ivy League school now. I think she's already drafting up a college essay for it." Tiana let out a small laugh that made Nate shiver.

"That's good," Nate lied.

Tiana let go of his hand and sat back in the chair, watching his face. "What's the matter? What's wrong?"

Nate looked at Tiana. He wanted to tell her everything, but he couldn't. They had come so far, and they had gotten away with it.

"I'm just worried about her." It was only half a lie. He was worried, but not about her. He was worried for everyone around her.

80

Ella
May 11, 2022

"Thank you for agreeing to meet me." Clemens sat across from Ella, who hid her eyes behind sunglasses. They were sitting at the same coffee shop she had met Tiana at years ago. A lot had happened in the past few days, and now that it felt like the air was finally clearing around her family, she felt better about the meeting. She hadn't invited Charlotte. In fact, she was hoping she would never have to speak to her again. After everything that happened, she was tinged with it.

Ella nodded but didn't offer Clemens a true reply. He took a sip of his coffee and set it down on the table. He had offered to get Ella one, but she refused. She didn't need coffee to keep awake these days—that happened naturally.

"I just wanted to start off by apologizing."

Ella's ears perked up, and she tilted her head slightly to the left.

"Investigations can be brutal and messy. I had to look at it from all the angles. I hope you can understand that."

Ella did since she herself had firmly believed that Nate might have been involved before Tony Holtz had shown up in her house with a gun. As she sat in the car with Sophia, she had become convinced. Maybe Nate came home, discovered his father was having an affair, and killed him and the mistress. Maybe he forced Ryan to take drugs before he did it. It wouldn't surprise her if Nate had access to drugs or even used them himself. Her mind flicked back to seeing him in the alleyway, the trash can on fire, his eyes lit up.

But all of that had been wrong.

Clemens shifted uncomfortably in his seat.

"I do," she finally replied.

"How is Nate doing?" he asked, shaking his head. "I should have asked that first."

"He got released yesterday. It was minor damage to his calf. Just have to take care of the wound until it heals completely."

Ella didn't have words to describe the immense relief she felt when the doctor told her Nate would be fine. She never thought her family would make it out of the house alive. But by some miracle, they had. It hadn't really been a miracle, though. It had been Sophia. She saved all of them.

"Good. That's really good." Clemens took another sip of his coffee. Based on the face he made, Ella decided he must not like it very much. "So, we have mostly concluded our investigation."

"I've heard." Ella had finally been able to watch the news coverage now that her family was out of the spotlight. Well, except for Sophia, that was. She was being praised on a few of the local stations as a hero for rescuing her family from a horrible home invasion. Ella had watched her self-confidence bloom as a result, and Ella figured that was a pretty big silver lining.

"Yeah, the news coverage has been pretty comprehensive. But basically, I wanted to let you know that we were able to find enough evidence linking Sam to this Tony guy. It looks like money was exchanged between them. The news hasn't gotten a hold of this yet, but it looks like maybe he was even an associate of Kelly Carter."

Ella leaned back in her chair. She hadn't expected that.

"Sam was?" she clarified.

"Him and Tony. We think Sam hired him and Kelly."

Ella's sunglasses shifted as she raised her eyebrows.

"Apparently, she wasn't the all-American girl her parents painted her to be." Clemens shook his head as if he saw it all the time. "At the end of the day, Nate had nothing to do with it. I am so glad for that."

Ella nodded. She couldn't tell him that she was too.

Clemens met her eyes for a moment too long, as if he was searching for her in the oversized sunglasses. She stared back before glancing away at the traffic traveling down the road.

"Anyway. I have a good feeling about it. I think Sam will be going away for quite a while, if not forever."

Ella swallowed hard. The potential that he could get out ever terrified her.

"He's currently cooperating with the investigation. That's why he may not get life."

Ella's head tilted to the side, and she finally lifted her sunglasses.

"Why would he do that?"

"Because he's guilty. Or because he doesn't want to risk the death penalty."

Ella frowned, thoughts swirling in her head. *Or he is protecting someone else.* She shook the thought away and pulled her purse into her lap.

"Thanks for meeting with me. It was—" Ella paused to find the right word. "Therapeutic."

A smile bloomed on Clemens's face, and Ella thought for the first time that if you gave him a white beard and matching hair, he almost looked like he could play Santa Claus. There was a jolliness about him that she had never really seen before. She wondered if he regretted getting into police work. It was about one of the grimmest careers you could choose.

"I'm glad, Mrs. Thomas." He stood up as she did and reached out his hand. She shook his and gave him a sweet smile. Having the police on your side was a good thing, she'd decided.

81

Nate
May 12, 2022

"What do you think?" Sophia asked, staring at Nate with big eyes. He blinked, trying to ignore the pain ruminating in his calf.

"It's good. Really good," he emphasized. The college essay she had crafted was the kind of thing they ended up producing movies about. The ones where they would say 'based off a true story' and Sandra Bullock played your mom. The ones where they showed pictures of the real you at the end. She wasn't foolish. That was for sure.

"I know," Sophia chirped, her energy exploding out of her. Her entire outlook had transformed in the past two weeks. She went from sobbing in the stairwell to sitting in their living room where a man had been shot three days prior, excited about her future. It was enough to give anyone whiplash. Except for her.

"It's too early to apply, right?" he asked. She was still only finishing up her sophomore year. College was a decent way off.

"Yes and no. I was talking to the guidance counselor at school—"

Nate wanted to interrupt her and ask when. She had only been in school two days since the shooting. It seemed a little too perfect. Just like everything she did.

"—and she said that if I enroll in some online courses this summer, I could start next year as a senior. That would mean applications would start in just a few months. I'm hopeful for early admission. She told me not to get my hopes up, but she winked after she said it. So, it's basically a sure thing."

Nate swallowed hard. There was a lump in his throat he just couldn't shake.

"What? Aren't you excited for me?" Her voice was demanding, and to Nate, frightening.

"Of course, I am." Nate's brain fumbled for an excuse. This one came easily enough. "It's just—you're going to do so great, and here I am, the permanent disappointment of the family. No plan. Nothing." It was true. He had always been the 'bad kid' in his parent's eyes. Apparently, Sophia and her father even had secrets that they hadn't shared with anyone else. He wasn't close to any blood relatives. So why had he been the only one crying that day?

"You'll figure it out." Sophia shrugged, her smile never leaving her face. "Besides, Mom will need someone here to look after her."

Nate nodded. It was better that the person doing that was him, even if he wasn't her first choice. It was safer.

"Hey," Sophia said. Nate's eyes snapped up from the carpet and locked on her clouded eyes. "This whole thing, it's better if we just forget about it, right?"

Nate bit his bottom lip and nodded.

Sophia stood up, closing the distance between them. She grabbed his jaw, forcing his face to look up at her roughly.

"It never happened. And if you think it did"—her grip tightened on his skin, and he wondered for a brief second if she would strangle him without a second thought—"I will make sure the whole world knows exactly what you did."

"It never happened," Nate agreed because there was no other choice.

EPILOGUE

Tiana
May 16, 2022

"How are you feeling with everything? Now that it's over," Tiana asked. They had agreed to one more session. At least, Ella and she had. Sophia was mostly a forced participant in this. Ella had argued that after killing a man, at least one therapy session was necessary.

Sophia shrugged. A pillow rested on her lap, and she had one arm casually wrapped around it.

"Good, actually."

Tiana adjusted in her seat, crossing her left leg over the right. She had a notepad sitting on her lap, but as usual, she wasn't writing anything. It was her own security blanket, something to fiddle with while she talked to patients.

"Really?" Tiana feigned surprise in her voice. Nate had told her that Sophia was actually rather excited about the turn of events, but hearing it firsthand was a whole other story.

"Yeah. I mean, I got what I wanted."

Tiana raised an eyebrow. "And that was?" She was pretty sure she already knew where this was going.

"Colleges are going to fight over me now. It's not a bad gig."

Tiana smiled widely. "It's always good to look at the silver linings."

"That's what I try to tell everyone else. But they don't always listen to me."

Tiana nodded. "People rarely listen to what I say too," she joked.

A smile spread on Sophia's face. "I tried to tell Sam that it could have been worse."

Tiana's eyebrows immediately flew together, and she cleared her throat involuntarily.

"What? You spoke to him?" Tiana had to admit she was surprised when Sam confessed to the murders and the disposal of Kelly Carter's body without exception. Nate wouldn't have admitted to moving the body if he had nothing to do with it. But at the same time, she had known all along he wasn't telling the whole truth. Sophia *must* have been there too. She spoke to them *both* on the phone at the same time that day. For some reason, Sam had taken the fall for all of it.

"Yeah. Why do you think he confessed to it all?" Sophia asked nonchalantly.

Tiana could feel her heart beginning to race, and she played with the corner of her notepad, growing increasingly uncomfortable.

"I—well I figured that he—"

"Did it?" Sophia finished. She shook her head, and Tiana felt a wave of coldness swallow her body whole.

She opened her mouth to speak, but she could no longer form words.

"He didn't want to tell people he did it. Of course not. He thought he still had a chance if it went to court. Circumstantial evidence can make it hard to win a case. But I convinced him otherwise."

Tiana blinked. "How?" The word came out hoarse, like it wasn't even her voice. She was scrambling to piece together what Sophia was truly saying.

"Well, you know they don't take kindly to pedophiles in prisons."

Tiana tilted her head to the side, wondering where she was going with this. Had Sophia been molested as a child? Was his confession in exchange for her silence?

"So, I told him if he didn't confess, I would tell everyone he molested me."

Tiana fumbled over her words. "Sophia, I am so sorry." Guilt flooded over her. How had she never noticed the signs?

"He didn't actually do anything like that."

"He didn't?" Tiana shook her head, clearly lost in the conversation.

"I just said I would tell people he did. He agreed." She shrugged again, and Tiana stared, unable to form a thought as Sophia's words swirled in her brain.

"It's not like he was innocent or anything. I don't feel any remorse, if that's what you're wondering."

Tiana licked her lips and forced herself back into her chair, unaware that she had been leaning forward. She clutched the notepad to stop her hands from shaking.

"What happened to your dad, Sophia?" The question surprised even Tiana. She hadn't meant to ask. She didn't truly want to know, but she couldn't help herself.

"That's between me and Nate."

Tiana shook her head. "Nate can't handle keeping that kind of secret." She wasn't sure if that was entirely true. He had kept most of the truth quiet so far, but parts had slipped up. He wasn't a bad-natured kid despite what everybody believed.

"He is going to have to." A sly smile spread across Sophia's face, and when Tiana blinked, she could still see it staring at her.

"Why?" Tiana asked. She was asking a lot with a single question. Why had Sophia let this happen? Why had she let everyone around her lie? Why would Nate keep her secret? Why did she force Sam to confess?

"It was the only way." Sophia rose to her feet now, grabbing her purse from the couch beside her. "I think we're probably done here."

Sophia took a step forward, and Tiana forced herself to stay in the chair. She wanted to get up and run, but she didn't want to seem skittish.

Sophia wrapped her arms around Tiana in a hug like they had done many times before. Tiana could feel hot breath on her neck as Sophia gripped her firmly.

"I wouldn't say anything to anyone . . .," Sophia murmured, her voice like a purr. "You know, Nate is in a very fragile state. If this were to come out, I'm not sure he would be able to handle it. Emotionally, you know." Sophia pulled back, the smirk still on her face. "I'll see you later!" Her voice had all the enthusiasm it had carried when she first walked in.

Tiana nodded, her lips shut tightly. Sophia turned and left, slamming the front door as she went.

ACKNOWLEDGMENTS

When I got ready to start writing *It Never Happened*, I thought it would be a lot easier to write a second book with one under my belt. I was sorely mistaken.

My greatest appreciation goes to my husband, who immediately pushed me to write a second book. I doubt that if I was married to anybody else that my dream of publishing a novel (let alone two) would have ever come true.

Sarah, my editor, thank you for always being the first to read my work and for making me feel a lot better about what I initially think is a jumbled mess. I am so lucky that you were my first choice in an editor because I wouldn't want anybody else. And a big thank you to Kelsea, my sensitivity reader, for helping me do justice to all my characters.

To my parents, thanks for supporting my dream and peddling my books to whomever you can.

Thanks to all my friends and coworkers who have bought my books, especially the ones that don't normally read.

And to all of you who just randomly stumbled upon my books, thank you for taking a chance on me.

ABOUT THE AUTHOR

Carley Wolfe spends her days listening to teenagers complain about American Literature and daydreaming about summer vacation. When she is not writing or eating good food, she is cuddling with her pets, and occasionally, her husband. *It Never Happened* is her second novel.

Made in the USA
Monee, IL
15 November 2023

46627105R00177